The *fragility* of

PRESSED FLOWERS

LINDA RUTH BROOKS

GUM TREE
press

A catalogue record for this book is available from the National Library of Australia

Fiction/social issues/contemporary romance

Cover, text design, typesetting & interior design by *Linda Ruth Brooks*
Photo artwork: *Linda Ruth Brooks*

ISBN: 978-0-6455650-9-6

The Fragility of Pressed Flowers and other books by Linda Brooks may be purchased through online bookstores and retail outlets

Author

Linda Brooks lives in Adelaide. She writes nonfiction, poetry, fiction and short stories. She has published and illustrated children's books. She has a BA Hons in Creative Writing from Southern Cross University. She gained a publisher for her childhood memoir *A Curious & Inelegant Childhood*. She has written a nonfiction book on living with Asperger's Syndrome *I'm not broken, I'm just different* and the children's book *Callan the Chameleon* with contributions from Professor Tony Attwood.

Published in anthologies: 'Coastlines' 5, 6, 7 & 8 by Southern Cross University; 'Wood, Bricks & Stone'; 'Grieve', 'Third Wednesday Poets' and 'Longing for Solitude'. Awards: Rebecca Coyle Scholarship for Hons; first prize for The Legacy University Level Creative Writing Award; first prize in the Gabe Reynaud Creative Writing Award and the Mater Misericordiae Grieve Writing Award.

A registered nurse and advocate for disability in a previous life, Linda has a rich background in listening to the stories of others, never shying away from the darker, gritty tales. And yet, humour is never far away. Linda enjoys hearing from her readers (even if they've found typos): lindaruthbrooks@bigpond.com

Author titles

Nonfiction:

I'm not broken, I'm just different
(on Asperger's with Professor Tony Attwood)
A Curious and Inelegant Childhood

Verse novel:

The day the war ended

Adult fiction:

Behind Whispering Hands
The Unprize
A broken hallelujah
Scarlett doesn't live here anymore
Under the Bracken Fern

Children's books:

A Tabby Never Forgets
Callan the Chameleon (Asperger's Syndrome)
Dusty Bunny's Very Important Job
Izzy & Pudding the Cat
I want a monkey!
Madam Iris Bigglesworth
The Banyula Tales - 6 stories
Who Stole Christmas?

Publisher of the anthologies:

We are Australian'
The Great Australian Shed
Waltzing Matilda

To Louise

Contents

The Street

It was the kind of street where kids moaned that nothing ever happened, but not to their parents who took anything approaching whingeing as an opportunity to make lists of chores and threaten to get a petition for the government to bring back child labour.

I was the kind of street where any resident would protest that they never gossiped and deplored anyone who did. This claim, made over fences and gates, was usually followed by an objective critique of all persons who weren't present at the time.

It was the kind of street where curtains twitched and everyone knew what everyone else was doing, and quite possibly much of what they might do in the future. This involved a great deal of social manoeuvring where a good memory and keen eye for random eavesdroppers who might break the careful rules of society by taking the tale back to the gossipee, which was a fate to be avoided at all costs because of the stress of the invention of the most acceptable little white lies. Oh no, I said nothing of the sort. How could you think that of me?

It was the kind of street where kids became bored with scraping sticks, rolling tyres and swapping marbles, being bereft of PlayStations and iPads. This led to children to becoming excessively interested in listening in to adult conversation. Or it might have just been me. I found that contrary to populist claims, a whole lot of stuff happened, things that would make Days of Our Lives look a bit tame. If one was paying attention of course, or, hiding in the treehouse while mothers "didn't gossip over the fence. All of this would be called network in the future.

It was the kind of street where a rotund church deacon took a constitutional after lunch, meandering to the other end of the street. Taking a small detour to the knotty gum tree, he reached into a crevice, found the whiskey bottle and took a tipple or three. Local boys who knew of his habit often availed themselves of a tipple or three themselves, replacing the alcohol with water in a reverse miracle of the wine at the wedding. At the intersection the garage owner was shot dead with a sawn-off shotgun by a certifiable dimwit who drove to the nearest café where he was arrested halfway through his burger and before he'd sampled his hot chips.

It was the kind of street that had a seldom used airstrip at one end where we hooned around in go-carts which I tried to convince my father had adequately prepared me to drive a car without lessons. He gave up. My then boyfriend, who was particularly adept at giving up, also gave up. Mum sent me to a driving instructor with a bad temper and deplorable manners, who called me a maniac if you please! There was the sibling incest that everyone for a fifty-mile radius knew about and cheerfully passed on. Another deacon with pleasant manners passed around the offering bag for the tithe-paying parishioners, went home with his wife and children, enjoyed lunch then had a nap ... with his girlfriend on the other side of town. There was a car theft, a jail term, shooting of streetlights. You see what I mean now, we're only up to the fifth paragraph and there's been adultery, alcoholism, theft, incest, vandalism and murder.

It was the kind of street that had an estimable cast of characters, enough to fill several Netflix sagas. An old, white-bearded man who resembled a dwarf scared children by telling them he would eat their pets. His wife always wore an apron and could have easily stepped off the pages of a Dickens' novel. There were the dainty old ladies who toiled in their garden and were always ready for a chat or an impromptu sandwich. One old darling had a dining chair for her cat. There was the builder who promised to fix us kids up with a swimming pool if we dug the hole. We managed mere inches. There was the woman who tatted while her husband caught tadpoles. The mad bastard who took his rattling rusty wheelbarrow to the corner store for groceries and repaired a dent in his car door with cement that fell off halfway down the street. His wife shrieked and screamed every day as cats and rats escaped through long grass and then tall fences to face the neighbour's .303. There were businesses in residential zoning—an electrical appliance shop, a second-hand car yard and a mechanics workshop.

It was the kind of street where women collected Artex paints then covered aprons and tablecloths, attended tedious cycles of Tupperware parties until their kitchens contained little else. Mothers bought camphor chests and kitchenware for the daughters' glory boxes, encouraging their offspring to marry up and not down. Terrified of unwanted pregnancies they lectured through all the daylight hours with never a thought of providing anything by the way of the facts of life that went beyond the film put on at the church hall, narrated by an elderly bespectacled woman with dour demeanour who delivered nothing more than a brief precis on farm animals. None of us had farm animals so we left as ignorant as we arrived and a good deal more confused. Just to be safe, we all swore off kissing, holding hands and sitting in a seat after a boy. The distinction between Drugs and Medicines was never defined because it was completely unnecessary for anyone to know in that kind of street.

The fragility of pressed flowers
Henry Street, QUIRINDI, 1955

Rain falls in soft, warm splatters, trembling like butterflies on the flowers of the grevilleas that edge our verandah where I sit on the bench-swing waiting for Nanna Ennis. We're going food shopping at McDonald's Corner Store. I wish she would hurry up. I'm wearing pink ballet shoes and tap my toes together. The bread delivery man passes on his way home. He toots and waves as I peek out from the shrubs. Mrs Kingston across the road at No. 4 is digging up daffodil bulbs, brushing them off with gardening gloves and putting them in her apron pocket. She keeps looking over here. I guess she's keeping an eye on me.

At last Nanna arrives, puffing and fiddling wither hat. Nanna has her going down the street clothes on. Her hair is pinned in a bun. She's wearing her second-best winter coat over a flowery dress. A thin blue belt has crept up under her bosoms because she's hasn't got a waist anymore.

Nanna tells me to hurry so we'll avoid the early-morning rush at McDonald's corner shop, but when we get there, she spies a few of her war-widow friends and starts to natter. She gives me the list and tells me not to dawdle while they huddle in the doorway, their hats almost touching.

Inside McDonald's shop, next to boxes of yellow-tapered candles, matches and rat traps there are two pairs of working boots. They're muddy and scuffed. They belonged to the McDonald's sons who died in the war. Mrs McDonald says she'll never clean those boots because her boys were wearing them on the last day she ever saw them.

Nanna doesn't approve of the boots. She calls them dead things and says they only bring sadness to people's minds. I don't remind her that she has an upstairs room full of dead things. I know because I poke around in there sometimes. Boxes and suitcases are packed in tight. There are tea chests with black stencilled signs like BUSHELLS, *Tea of Flavour* with names in Nanna's handwriting. One box has *David William Ennis*, my mum's brother. He was killed in France. They couldn't bring his body home so he's buried over there and Nanna has a tea chest that's nailed shut.

As long as I can remember Nanna Ennis has been in charge of our house. Even when Mum was alive and went away.

Mum died four years ago. I'd just turned six and started school. Nanna didn't think I should be around Mum when she was dying. The day Mum died Dad disagreed with her and brought me home from school to say goodbye. He picked me up in the school bus he drove because we didn't have a car. Mum was lying on the daybed near the window, listening to the magpies' song and fighting to breathe. I kissed her forehead. It was damp and waxy. Mum squeezed my hand, then closed her eyes, as if she'd fallen asleep.

After Mum died, I loved going to her room—to touch her clothes, slip on her shoes, dap her 4711 perfume on my wrist, like she did, and remember her. I'd press her silver hairbrush with its strands of blonde hair against my cheek. Mum had her own room, even before she got sick with cancer, and after she died it was the only place that still had her scent.

Then one afternoon, a few months after Mum died, I opened the door to find everything different. None of Mum's things were there. There wasn't one blonde hair anywhere. Not even the dust was left behind, just a horrid smell of disinfectant. Nanna.

I ran up Henry Street to Nanna's place, crying angry tears. Across George Street, the main street, without looking for traffic. Past Mr Evans as he lifted the canvas flap on his vegetable truck.

Nanna was putting out the fire under the copper in the laundry. Her sleeves were rolled up and her face was red and sweaty.

'What have you done with Mum's things?' I started throwing wet washing on the floor, looking for anything of Mum's. Her scent would be washed off everything.

'*Lucy Meredith Carter!* Stop that! I gave them away. You can't keep dead things.'

I screamed, 'You're a dead thing, Nanna!'

Dad came panting through the door with the long bits of his hair on the wrong side.

'What possessed you to do that, Ethel?' He put his hair back on the right side. 'The child only wanted something of her mother's.'

I walked straight out of Nanna's house. Past the cabinet where she keeps Grandpa's old pipe. Past the black cast-iron doorstop—the iron her mother used, wishing she understood.

Under the daybed Dad found a suitcase of Mum's, from when she used to go away. There wasn't much—a silk-embroidered notebook and a headscarf, but no strands of hair. Mum's scent had gone.

I sat sobbing on the bench-swing Dad built for us. Mum wasn't a hugging sort of mother, but there she'd brush my hair while she told me stories about her childhood with Fliss in the big house on Henry Street. Sitting there I wanted to remember every one of those minutes together. I wanted to forget all the times Mum went away.

Sometimes the memory of Mum leaving is stronger than the memory of her.

I still have Mum's silk embroidered notebook. It will never be a dead thing to me.

Under Mum's name, I wrote:

Lucinda Meredith Carter: Book of Known Facts. The notebook had wildflowers inside, pressed and dried, their petals as dainty as insect wings. Dad carefully brushed the flowers into a shoe box for safekeeping.

That's about all I remember.

I don't know where Mum went when she went away. No one wants to talk about that. If I ask questions, Nanna rambles about "the can't be said", and "the shouldn't be said". Someday I'll get things figured out.

I write things down in Mum's silk embroidered notebook so my stories don't get lost.

So many people have lost their stories. I imagine them drifting through the air like cloud words where a sad story might bump into a celebration story and say, 'I do beg your pardon, I'm not quite myself at the moment.'

The air in some places must be crowded with them.

I have lost stories.

If I keep track of facts, they might fit into my story.

It's September. Nanna's wisteria is covered in blossoms. Mauve flowers hang like bunches of grapes. 'How odd,' says Nanna. 'They haven't bloomed for years.'

'They have, Nanna. You just haven't seen them. You're usually up with Great-Aunt Bea at this time of the year.'

A horn parps in the street. Nanna looks at her watch.

'Oh, that's your father already. We best get moving. Bea will be here soon. I'll get my hat and coat.'

Nanna's sister, Great-Aunt Bea, is as plump as the ripe yellow peaches she brings every year in waxy brown boxes from Bathurst. Smelling of Lily of the Valley and cigarette smoke from the train, Great-Aunt Bea plants whiskery kisses on my cheeks.

She hands a basket of peaches to the curved-back railway attendant who unloads her cases.

'For your kind self, good sir,' she says.

With the radio blaring, pans clattering, she takes over Nanna's kitchen. Glass bottling jars rattle in pots of boiling water. Rich ripe fruit bubbles on the stove. Sweet syrupy smells fill the room. Soon, there's sticky pink and purple juice on aprons, benches and even misted on windowpanes. After cooling, bottles are lined up carefully on shelves Dad built in the outdoor laundry.

Great-Aunt Bea takes me with her to visit Fliss at Montview, choosing a day Nanna has an all-day CWA meeting. I'm glad of that. Without Nanna there I might be able to do the thing that Nanna hates; ask questions.

In spite of her poor dragging leg, Great-Aunt Bea insists on walking to Montview to visit Mum's sister, Fliss. Fliss lives at the convalescent home on account of having a stroke and losing all her words.

I'm surprised when the orphaned Pieter brings a tea tray, setting it down carefully on a small table. He usually stays far away from people, rarely smiling, scowling at us kids. He's only been in Australia a while.

Great-Aunt Bea thanks Pieter as if he's a butler in a palace.

Pieter nods formally. Then Aunt Bea pours the tea, chatting to Fliss as if it's a perfectly normal conversation between two people. 'Now, Fliss—How often do you get out of this place, dear?'

Fliss shrugs. Great-Aunt Bea sighs. 'As I thought.'

She pulls on her gloves and has a quick word with Pieter. A taxi arrives. We're going shopping!

Great-Aunt Bea buys lovely, girly things for Fliss: Pears soap, perfume, nighties and slippers. While Pieter pushes Fliss' wheelchair, Great-Aunt Bea slips away, reappearing with a brown paper parcel.

On the porch swing at our house, while Dad prepares afternoon tea, I read to Great-Aunt Bea from my Book of Known Facts. 'Your dad told me about this marvellous book,' she says, winking at Dad through the kitchen window.

Esmeralda sits on the swing, pecking at sunflower seeds while we eat biscuits and drink tea. I tell Great-Aunt Bea it's just as well Nanna is away because she can't take to chooks being pampered, magic or not.

Great-Aunt Bea tut-tuts and says, 'It's never been proved which creatures are magic and which aren't, so I'm keeping an open mind on the subject.' She nods at Dad who brings the brown paper parcel. It now has a soft pink bow.

Inside is a large square book that has the thinnest, finest pages I've ever seen. 'What is it?' I ask.

We sit around the kitchen table. Dad brings out a shoe box. Mum's pressed wildflowers are still pretty and bright, still as dainty as butterfly wings.

Great-Aunt Bea's hands aren't steady enough so Dad gets a tiny pair of tweezers and carefully places each flower on a pure white page. I try, but it's much harder than it looks when I try.

When we're finished Great-Aunt Bea claps her hands.

She stays for another week, when a wheezing bout of asthma sends her scuttling back to the cool, dry mountain air of Bathurst. When she leaves the ground is covered with fallen wisteria petals.

- From *The lost stories of Lucy Meredith Carter.*

Doll

(Wherever the wind blows)

In the days before Keely went mad, seduced by the security of insanity, the blur of it, it was summer all the time. It's not summer now and I don't know where Keely is. After those early days our friendship stopped and started before finally jerking to a halt.

I sit in the still evening, in the nook by the open fire that is flanked by two bookshelves overstuffed with books. There's a braided hippy rug that slips and bunches on the timber floors. Not my style, yet it keeps the chill from bare feet. Yesterday's newspaper is on the side table. The local café owner at the end of the street leaves a copy of the previous day's paper on a corner table for me when I arrive for breakfast. I'm not a fan of news, but the paper is a generosity, and the crossword on page 2 is an obsession. The front-page screams yesterday's news, a fatality at the local rail station, not far from here. I flip it over.

I chose this two-bedder flat because I fell in love with it. Something you're never supposed to do. Especially in leafy suburbs where prices are high. When the pinch came for the mortgage I let the other bedroom to a young couple, seasonal workers, currently off picking stone fruit. Their boho style is scattered among my classic conservatism. The rug is theirs. Keely would have loved it, but we haven't spoken in a decade.

I don't know why, after ten years, I'm thinking of Keely. Our meetings were always unexpected. Chance encounters. We'd bump into each other, rushing to do whatever business we had. It didn't matter how long it had been, or how upset we'd been with each other, we'd laugh and hug. Whatever stood between us was forgotten, if only for a while. We were Keely and Kate again.

The telephone lines hum with cyber chatter, replacing the personal, the sound of someone's voice. The ancient woman in the adjoining flat is dragging her rattan chairs out of the rain that hasn't come. She senses it looming. I don't dare scoff. She is so often right.

A clap of thunder shivers the house. A fierce wind roars. Ignatius, the most aloof cat on earth, bolts across me in a black and orange streak, seeking to hide in my walk-in-robe. There's a thumping sound. I wonder if the old woman is in trouble, but the noise grows louder. It's the heavy front door knocker.

A long, bulky trench coat flaps erratically in the rain-drenched wind, parting briefly to reveal generous feminine curves. The coat is a designer style, a soft Khaki, although stained by the torrential rain. I think the woman says something, but I can't be sure. The coat flies open.

Sheltered in its folds is a child, a girl, with wide green eyes and rampant brown curls.

The woman's voice is lilting. I still can't make out the words. Or the intent. That changes when she pushes the child through the doorway. The girl stumbles on the stoop and wraps herself around me to avoid falling.

'Oops,' she says, seemingly unnerved by the storm or the stranger in front of her.

The storm takes a breath.

The woman speaks. I hear her words clearly now. 'You always said you would.'

I lean forward. There's a wisp of red hair.

Keely.

I reach out an arm to drag her in, but she turns. I glance down at the child. When I look up there's no sign of Keely. Staccato lightning flashes, illuminating the street. Nothing. Not even a stray dog.

There's a stone in my throat. The intersections of our lives were always unexpected, but this?

The child tugs on my dressing gown.

'Keely said I have to stay with you.' She walks into the flat with a little girl swagger as if everything has been satisfactorily explained and settled.

'Hadn't you better close the door?' she says, shedding a miniature backpack and her own small trench coat, the same fabric and style as Keely's.

Her name, she tells me, is Doll. She is nearly eight years old. Her tone is matter of fact and her only sign of anxiety is her need for a phone. Do I have one? A mobile? Any sort?

She grabs it eagerly. Nimble fingers flit across the screen. There's an animated stream of words.

I wait to join in the call, arm outstretched, hoping for some adult conversation or explanation. Anything that would make sense of this night.

Doll ends the call.

'I left a message,' she says.

'Oh. A message? I thought...'

I find a pen and notepad, ask rapid fire questions. Who, when, where?

Doll presses stiff fingers into her forehead. 'Uh ... I dunno ... I live everywhere and nowhere. Mostly in between.' An escaping tear is brushed aside quickly. 'I'm not supposed to cry.'

In between. Keely's vagrant child.

'It's okay.' I hug her. She melts into me. I feel her body tremble.

Ignatius comes out of hiding, tail aloft, mortal panic due to thunder a distant memory. He winds himself around the girl's legs. A well-practised tactic that yields its usual reward. Doll claps her hands. 'Ooh, a kitty. I love kitties.'

'He likes you too.'

'What's his name?' She bends down to stroke the cat's motley fur.

'Ignatius.'

'I've always wanted a kitty of my own. You're so lucky Kate.'

'How did you know my ... name?' I ask, but the child is either beguiled by the cat or ignoring my questions. I tense as a frisson of annoyance rises.

I turn to the practicalities. 'Have you eaten?'

'Thought you'd never ask.' Doll sits on the sofa and pats her tartan pleated skirt gingerly. Satisfied with its dryness she unwinds a matching scarf from around her neck and says, 'phew'.

I let her feed Ignatius.

My hands are shaking. The contents of the fridge fail to inspire. I order pizza. I tear the cardboard top in two and hand half to her as a plate. She devours the oozing pizza slices with finger-licking delight.

When she's done, she wipes her hands on a masculine looking handkerchief that apparently belongs to Darda.

'Do you live with Darda?' I ask, my tone neutral. I don't want to spook her again.

'Hmm. Sometimes.'

'Is Darda your father?'

She giggles. 'No silly. He's *Uncle* Darda. I don't stay there long. His wife has nerves.'

'Oh,' I say. 'That's ...'

'Enough about me,' she says, sounding thirty, 'what about you? *Specifically* you and Keely.' She wriggles back into the recliner chair opposite me, folds her arms and waits, my cooperation a foregone conclusion.

Keely and I went everywhere together. Often with friends: hiking, swimming, art shows, markets, evening gourmet picnics with campfires on the beach. The two of us would take long meandering road trips that began and ended on a whim.

We attended the same school. Keely was the bright cityscape to my dull country life, the colours of the carnival to my bushland lanes, bringing vivid life to a grey background. I had never been so wonderfully included, I, Kate, the bookish one, the library geek spouting Shakespeare and Donne.

We were oil and water. Keely was a curvaceous English rose, a foil to my Portuguese heritage and beanpole figure. Keely fell in and out of love like a whirlwind. Unlike me, with my slow burn.

On sailing trips Keely would be kitted out in jaunty mariner fashion, arms waving, short raffish hair dyed a stylish red. On the beach she'd be glamorous in a bright bejewelled caftan that would have hung on me like a tent. She'd have her arm around her latest in a string of ardent admirers, while both elegant hands wove a story of fantastical elements.

She was a masterful storyteller, and to my surprise, universally believed. I watched her, my mouth twitching, as she narrated an endless repertoire of amazing adventure. Many were dreadful tragedies, yet Keely never carried the air of A Tragic. That way, her listeners were spared the burden of pity for her.

I have never met anyone like her.

I pause, unsure of how much to reveal to the child. I'm at a loss.

'It's September,' I say, wishing I knew if it was school holiday time, wondering why Keely was nearby with her daughter.

This precocious child may be accustomed to the life of a gypsy, but I am not. I didn't even know Keely had a child, a symptom of my estrangement from that group of friends, and that dreadful time. That gut-wrenching decision I've never spoken of. How could I?

I hope the child will have more to say. She knows more about me than I of her. 'Doll,' I begin. 'Tell me about you.'

Her response is an indecipherable murmur. Her eyes slowly droop. She snuggles further down the recliner, where Ignatius, the traitorous puss, who has never sat anywhere near me, curves into her arms.

I check my mobile. The number has disappeared, that is, if Doll phoned anyone at all. Has she learned the art of fiction from her mother? A hard ball of worry unsettles me. The past has returned and it's an uncomfortable guest.

Our third year in high school was the year Keely and I both changed. That year was a fractured thing, a torn scrap of a year that anyone in their right mind would have ignored as best they could, and moved on.

It was the year I grew up.

My brother went to gaol. Something that never happened in our small town, to people like us, to our family. Our lives splintered into a kind of mute isolation from the community where every greeting was hastily and awkwardly curated, before silence.

My mother's grief was so profound that she never left the house. My father and I filled the gaps. Shopping, washing, cleaning. Childhood was no more.

It was the year Keely went wild.

Her family moved to the other side of the world to the exotic landscapes and cities of Europe. Dislocated, Keely ran away, disappearing for days then weeks at a time.

My disappearance was far more subtle. No one saw the change. Not even I.

Years passed before Keely and I met again. Newly returned from overseas she was a colourful cosmopolitan creature. If I was pressed, even now, I could not recount the chronology of her life after our school years despite hearing her stories. Those harmless, entertaining yarns of exotic places and perilous catastrophes.

The dangers of backpacking alone and penniless across Europe. A lucky escape from Somali pirates. Part of a purse-snatching gang in Italy. Falling in love at every turn. Held hostage in a hut in a Tibetan mountaintop. At every new occasion fresh narratives emerged, each darker and more outrageous than the last. Her audiences were spellbound. She shone.

I realised Keely herself was the truest, most fervent believer of her tales. Had she become the story, not just the storyteller?

While the child sleeps, I check her backpack, feeling like an intruder. There's a notebook. It contains a variety of small flowers, pressed childishly between the pages. A strawberry lip gloss has leaked. There are snack wrappers and discarded chip bags, melted cheese sticks, a multi-coloured pen, some torn bread crusts, popcorn, movie ticket stubs and a small teddy bear on a keychain—with no key.

There is nothing of any practical value. Nothing to reveal a life.

There's a tap on the sliding door at the back of the unit. The old woman is standing there, yellow-coated against the slanting rain. Avoiding a puddle in the courtyard we share. She has a small bunch of flowers—her usual ploy to pry into my life. She smiles and hands me the sweet peas.

'Child out on a night like this,' she says. 'Irresponsible.'

'She's not ... lost. Her mother brought her here.'

The woman's face contracts in a telling moue. 'If you say so.'

I flinch as an icy wind blasts between us.

'Child out on a night like this.' She yanks her raincoat around her. Gives me a warning stare. She's never forgiven me for the time I had the preschool children over for a party. The only time she had to endure what she calls Unnecessary Noise. She knows I left the job years ago. When my husband tired of waiting for a child of his own and departed with a younger, fertile version who was already inexplicably pregnant. 'Priorities,' he said, placing me firmly outside that category.

'The child is fine. I've known her mother for years.'

I shrug and inch the door to hint that our conversation should end. The exchange has chilled me as much as the invading wind.

The old woman snorts and stomps off. Leaving me with the past and its taut confusion.

I remember summer activities on cold winter days where Keely's kitchen was a paradise of aroma, flavour and colour. Those normal moments where her unpredictability receded, leaving me wondering if I had imagined it all.

And yet, the gap between reality and fantasy widened. There were strange midnight calls, with Keely urgent, terrified. 'Please come, Kate.' Yet when I'd arrive, she'd claim no memory of the frantic call. She'd pat me, feed me and send me on my way. Borrowed clothes went unreturned. Conversations were erased by some gremlin in her brain. Past loves and narratives were replaced with new ones. If I mentioned former stories, Keely gave me a pitying look. I was the crazy one.

I distanced from her. Her stories were no longer harmless. She began spreading confidences far and wide, often repeating the stories of others, enlarging and making them her own. She broke things and people.

Pushing these thoughts aside I make a pot of tea. The dilemma of what to do now is far more pressing. How many times have I retraced those memories? A quest that always ends with questions; not answers. Now I have her cherry-cheeked daughter sleeping on my sofa. Doll still wears her tartan skirt, her purple fingerless gloves, as if departure might be necessary at any moment.

A child out on a night like this.

I don't know where Keely is or what she intends. I only know that the Keely I remember would never abandon her child. Keely will return.

When my teacup is empty, I sit on the sofa near Doll's head. I touch the dark curls.

The child snores. A sound intolerable in husbands and

boyfriends but endearing in a child. I sleep. When I wake my arm is tingling from the weight of a tousled head. Doll and Ignatius, the standoffish cat, are entwined.

The morning arrives with an exuberant sun that has already dried the remnants of last night's storm.

Yesterday's chill has been replaced with sticky summer heat. The child's clothes are totally unsuitable.

On waking, Doll is not the nonchalant child of yesterday.

She stares at me, drags in a sigh. 'It wasn't a dream then.'

'No, Cutie-patootie.'

She's as surprised as I by the endearment. She pulls at her tangled curls, looks at mine. 'We could be twins,' she says.

There's a hint of a smile when I suggest that breakfast is far more important than hair that doesn't behave.

'Shopping?' I ask.

'Shopping. It's been absolutely ages.'

As we walk to the shops a small hand searches for mine, and grips it. An unexpected rush of warmth embraces me, fighting with tired memories of defeat, of barren incompetence, failure and emptiness. The tests, the monitoring, the hope, and then arguments, tension and separation. Distancing from friends with children and their complaints of sleepless nights and tantrums was a feeble path to coping. I left my job at the preschool. I avoided even the vista of happy families, children's squeals, parental joy. Babies in prams outside supermarkets. Sights that stirred foot-shuffling despair.

Yet now, the universe has brought me a fleeting glimpse of what might have been. A moment of flinching joy, so soon to be wrenched away. By the capricious gods of chance. As we dawdle through pristine shops and gaze at delectable things behind shiny glass I daydream about what it would be like to have this precious being. The traitorous thought constricts my throat.

'I love this slow shopping,' Doll says, swinging my arm with hers. 'It's like eating ice-cream that never melts.'

We buy things for Doll. A sundress. Only one. I cannot claim this child. Sandals, leggings, a skirt. I buy her a small purse, put some coins in it, for her to choose and spend. She buys a toy for Ignatius.

Women smile and stop. 'What a lovely mother and daughter. What a happy pair,' they say.

Screeching of tyres, horns blaring, and city traffic bring me back to earth. There are things I should know. Now that I have her trust will Doll have more to reveal? Lunch of hot chips and milkshakes in a corner booth provide a conducive ambience.

Doll eats with her fingers, sliding the chips through tomato sauce. I do the same.

'Um, does...' I begin.

Doll interrupts. 'Keely does this a lot. You know. Drops me here and there. Mostly with people I've met before. Sometimes I even like them, but you're the best. Most people don't listen to kids. They speed up, give you lots of things you don't want. They make a fuss trying to fit you in. It never works. The other kids poke and pinch, just to let you know they'd rather you were somewhere else, things nobody sees, nobody hears.' Doll slurps on the straw. 'Sometimes Keely goes to hospital, you know. Special hospitals for people with, I dunno,' she waves her arm. 'Then I don't see her for a while.'

'Where have you been ... lately?' I ask.

'On an adventure. That's what Keely said. We saw exciting things at awesome places.' Doll makes an expansive gesture with her hands. 'I mean, like, we might have even seen the whole world. I dunno. We didn't have maps or anything. We saw colourful fish in a huge aquarium. We saw people acting on a big high stage. We went on ferries, and trams with wires on top.' She purses her lips. 'Hurry, hurry, hurry. The Hurry Holiday. That's what I call it. That's the way it is with Keely. Things are always changing.'

I hold my breath. Sit on the edge of the bench seat. I haven't the courage to ask the question on my mind. Was Keely coming to see me? Instead I say, 'so things change...'

'Yeah, like, things get faster and faster. They always do. But this time they got darker as well. Keely said we could only travel at nighttime. We stopped seeing nice places, having nice food. I asked why we couldn't stop somewhere but she whispered about danger and stuff. I got scared. She threw the phone away. Said people might listen. Might be after us. That she has dangerous secrets other people want. Important secrets. Secrets that she doesn't tell me, but in her sleep she mumbles a lot.'

Doll bites her lip. A vulnerable gesture. For the first time

I realise how much the child is seeking to please.

'She always comes to get me. Always.'

I suggest we walk home. Doll stops to pick every small flower she sees. I smile. Many of them are probably weeds.

'I'll make these last,' she says, 'they have to be pressed.'

My throat tightens. Permanence.

We pass the preschool where I once worked. The children are in the yard playing. Daniel, a chubby boy I cared for runs to the fence. I greet him.

'Hi Miss Kate,' he says. A friend calls him. Over his shoulder he yells, 'when are ya coming back?'

'Figures,' says Doll, shrugging. 'You're good with kids. Yep, you should.'

'Should what?'

'Go back.'

'I have a job.'

'But you hate it.'

'How do you know that Miss Bossy?'

'You looked so sad when I came.'

I steer Doll towards a lane. She gives me a quizzical look. Tilts her head. I laugh. We turn a corner and hear the rush of the surf, smell the salt air.

'Wow, Kate. You have a beach. Wow.'

We run along the edge of the bubbling surf. I show her how to tuck her dress into her undies, something she declares to be "wicked". We fall giggling onto the sand.

'Ooh,' says Doll, digging her toes into the wet sand.

'I love you,' she says. 'Because you called me Cutie

Patootie.'

I laugh. What a funny reason for loving someone.

'Same,' I say.

I show her my spinning beach dance. She spins too, singing, 'Wherever the wind blows, it can never catch me, but la la, la la free, something. Wherever the wind blows, that's where you'll find me.'

It's a simple composition, so familiar it constricts my chest. A memory. A guitar strummed in the flickering light of a dozen or more campfires, years ago.

Keely's song.

Nightmares tear my sleep apart. In brilliant colour, like a cartoon episode of *The Adventures of Tin Tin,* I see Keely and Doll, jumping into fast speed boats, leaping from rock to rock along a jagged cliff face, sleeping in corners, running down rain-soaked alleys. Keely discards things as they go, phones, keys, sanity. As I fight towards wakefulness, I hear her say, 'I'm immortal'.

Doll is sprawled sideways in my bed. I source slippers and gown. It's 2:00am. The witching hour. I boil the kettle and grab it before it whistles. Ignatius joins me. He purrs and leans into me. A change for the grumpy puss.

It's time I faced The Terrible Thing. That awful time that drove Keely and I apart for good.

It was a blustery night, as wild as Keely's most chaotic stories. Another phone call. Another cry for help. I had vowed to ignore them but the hysteria in her voice compelled me into action. Keely's disjointed words fought with static. She must have been outside, perhaps with the phone on speaker. Every sound seemed underwater.

I threw on a coat and left quickly, still wearing my preschool clothes with paint splatters, vegemite smears and blackcurrant juice stains.

It was a long drive.

Night mist shrouded the yard. Hearing Keely's low moaning I ran. She was naked on the concrete steps to her small apartment. Her skin was blue. Crouched around herself, she shook a fist at two policemen standing at a safe distance.

'Glad to see you. Friend of yours?' a burly officer asked.

I nodded. I looked around for something to hide her nakedness.

A summer storm threatened in the distance. The ground was muddy from an earlier drenching.

The cop came closer, leant towards me. 'She's been evicted. She's rambling about having paid rent, too much rent. But it's been to court.' He waved a paper. 'We didn't expect this malarkey. She threw her clothes off and burnt 'em.' He pointed to a sooty pile. 'She's raving about Interpol, the Feds, conspiracies, and some nonsense about being immortal. Drugs, or some doomsday cult.'

'Neither of those,' I said. 'I've never seen her like this. I mean she has some crazy ideas, but I've never heard her raise her voice.' Shaken from the change in Keely I grabbed a blanket from my car boot.

'She won't let us near her. We can't leave her like this. Phoned the ambos. Just waiting for 'em.'

The storm arrived with hoarded fury. I tried to put the

blanket around Keely, but she rejected it with a shriek. Her hair was matted. Soft brown roots showed it had been months since she dyed it.

Lightning flashed blue light on Keely. She looked blankly at me. Threw herself at me, then puked dark bile. Had she even been eating? I pulled the blanket tightly around her. Held her. She whimpered, soft mewling sounds.

The ambulance arrived. The trolley struggled with the muddy driveway.

'I'm coming with her,' I said, dispensing with my vomit-caked coat and shoes. Mud stuck to my feet. My hair was drenched, frizzy. I clambered up into the front seat of the ambulance.

Keely was strapped in the back. The screaming began again. She reached for me, thin hands slicing the air in futility. 'I will never forgive you!'

At the Accident and Emergency Department Keely was dazed by hospital fluorescence. Quietened by sedatives. She was quickly assessed for transfer to the psychiatric unit the next day.

Her sister and father arrived. Keely's father took in my bare feet, wild hair and tear-stained eyes. 'You'd better leave, Kate. We're here now. You will only make things worse.'

Keely looked angelic and composed in white hospital robes. I looked like a demented vagrant. Useless words croaked from my dry throat. Raw words that rasped and cut. 'But I ... She needed me. She called me.'

He blocked the space between me and Keely.

I left; bare feet silent along the hospital corridor.

I visited the next day. Tiptoed past the lounge room where her sisters and mother sipped steaming coffee from hospital cups. Their lips pursed precisely, whispering politely as good breeding dictated. Their privilege. Privilege that would forever exclude me. I would no longer be tolerated.

Keely sat unbound on a chair, beautifully dressed, hands folded delicately in her lap. She stared at me with watery blue eyes as if she didn't know what to make of me.

I was merely a part of a grey background. A world she no longer recognised, or required. She didn't know me. She didn't know anything, the nurses said, not even her hairbrush.

I have slept in. With my dressing gown half on, I yawn my way into the kitchen. The table has been set awkwardly. Ignatius sits patiently on a kitchen chair, waiting for his young worshipper to attend to his culinary needs.

Doll has a tea-towel draped over an arm. She asks what Madam would like for breakfast. I laugh and sink into a chair.

Partway through our cereal my mobile rings. We both freeze. It's an unwelcome intrusion. Dreaded. Doll pales and pushes her plate away. She stares at the floor.

It's Darda. The garbled phone message left by Doll has been received by his wife, but not understood. He's been away for a fortnight. Corporate seminars. He's brief. He'll arrive tomorrow. Early. I text my address.

Tomorrow.

Doll runs into the walk-in-robe, shrinks into Ignatius' favourite corner, and sobs. She turns her head away when I try to soothe her. 'I'm sorry it wasn't your ... Keely,' I say.

'It's not that,' she sobs, 'I want to stay with you. I don't want to live in between. A kid should be able to live in one house. I don't want to live with *everyone*. I want to live with you.'

I sit near her. I should be brave and wise, but there's a pain in my chest. 'Let's make memories,' I say, 'cupcakes? Pink frosting?'

'Always pink.'

The kitchen is a mess. We fill in the day. We play board games and cards, making up our own rules.

When dusk falls Doll sleeps with her arms around my neck.

When sunrise breaks the day open, I wash and fold her clothes. I put them in my carry-on case. I can always buy another. I can't bear to hand the child over with things in garbage bags. Something that apparently happens to unwanted foster kids.

Doll refuses breakfast. She sits on the sofa, legs swinging listlessly, with Ignatius wrapped like a baby in a throw rug on her lap.

I look at the calendar. I have been lost in the passing of days. It's been a week. How can life change so much in such a short time?

Darda shakes rain from his hair, oblivious of spraying me. 'Hello, Kate?'

I speak. But my words are too fast. They make no impression on the man. Occasionally he offers a smile that slips from his face as if wrenched by gravity. It unnerves me. His eyes scan the room. 'Ah, there you are Doll.'

He needs a quiet word with her. If he may. I offer the courtyard, hoping the old woman doesn't intrude past a flutter of curtain spying.

I hear a childish whimper, then sobbing. Ignatius squeezes through the cat door to Doll where he is welcomed with a crushing embrace.

Darda returns to the loungeroom. He hands me a newspaper. 'I stopped at the café down the street. When the owner knew I was on my way here he gave me this. Said he was worried about you. Hadn't seen you for a while. Understandable of course. With everything going on.'

I stare at the paper. "Rail Tragedy. Victim's Identity Revealed. Victim pushes a child to safety on a crowded platform, then falls to her death, crushed by the 5:10pm train." There's a photo.

Keely.

My legs buckle. I collapse on the sofa.

'Oh, sorry. You didn't know? I didn't mean to shock you. Are you alright?' He takes a step forward, then retreats. 'Um, of course Keely wanted you to have guardianship of Doll. That promise you made each other way back when.' He pulls a large beige envelope out of his coat. 'Here's the paperwork. Last Will and Testament. That sort of thing...'

A promise on a beach. A vow. A furious wind. An open door. A flash of red hair. A pair of gloved hands. A child in my arms.

Darda clears his throat. 'What I don't understand,' he says, 'is how the kid got here from the station.' Lacking a response, he leans forward and raises an eyebrow. 'I mean it must be seven ks at least.'

I shrug.

Soldatenkaffee Madeleine

At the Soldatenkaffee Madeleine on the Rue St Honoré a slender woman sits on the edge of a vinyl chair. Soldiers of the Reich are few this morning, after a beer-swilling, bawdy ballad party held in the Les Folies Belleville, then carried back to the Soldatenheim on Place Saint-Michel in the 6th arrondissement.

Those members of the Wehrmacht present this morning quietly contemplate their morning repast, paying minimal attention to the waitresses, usually the targets of their lusty overtures. Perhaps it's the previous night's numerous entertainments, or the presence of a senior SS officer that subdues them.

Elise Reynaud gathers the worn ermine collar of her coat to her slim neck. Soft young hands capture corded purse straps with taut tenderness.

She waits, indifferent to the aromatic wisps that escape the coffee machine. The Soldaten at the counter with their curious eyes do not exist for her. The hum of the early morning clientele, the murmurings of the barista and the hiss of steam as he tilts and creates, all of these are the backdrop to her leaning into anticipation.

Even the foreground, the busy street, is somehow slowed, the sounds of the traffic dulled.

It is but the stage for her meeting. She waits, leaning gently into the scene before her.

He is late. It worries her, for he is hardly ever late. But then, no other rendez-vous has been as important as today's. For this is the day they will leave Paris. The day they will claim their freedom, their future.

She glances at the suitcase, locked between her knees under the table, out of sight, banded tight with leather straps, ready for flight. Ready for him. The fragrance of his urgent kisses reignites her longing as she grips the handbag. He will come. He has never let her down. Not like the others. She blinks and refuses to think of them, of that.

She sees him, heart clenching as she recognises his long strides. His flapping charcoal coat, is unbuttoned and careless against the bitter wind. He presses his dark fedora down to shield his face from early stabs of rain as he crosses the road.

A truck passes, hiding him from view. She presses tense fingers against the glass, resisting the urge to leap to her feet and draw attention to her angst.

His smile—just one glimpse of his smile and all will be well. Her eyes scan rapidly, wishing the now rhythmic slant of rain aside, away.

The sullen quiet of the day ruptures. The world is chaos.

When the smoke clears, but before hearing returns, Elise

stares

Why didn't she hear the air raid siren?—the juddering of those engines in the sky?—the searing whistle of their deadly cargo?

Cathedral

A tall woman with a bright yellow umbrella stepped through the ornate cathedral doors. A taupe, tailored coat clung to her lean body. She grasped the lapels to shake off the rain. She had expected a parish sort of person to be in attendance, a priest or a canon, if that's what they were called. A sombre human presence of some sort, gliding with holy grace down the long aisles, waiting for the penitent, or the wayward.

Charlotte Bragg was neither and yet she hadn't been attracted to the church merely because it was the only shelter from the driving autumn rain. Directions from the divine was a fine concept but they had been in short supply in her seventy years of living on planet Earth. No, she was there to check out the church. The place where she would be unwelcome at this time tomorrow.

Outside the storm raged on. The flashes of lightning behind the coloured glass produced a magnificent display. She stared at the opulence of the place, the ragged garments of the porcelain Christ and she wondered about the poor, the confused, the lost, and the homeless, who would give anything to sleep on the comfort of a pew.

She would make a third-rate Catholic. In fact, if church attendance was a guide, then she would make a pretty poor showing in any religion. She never knew what to put on the Census form and each year there seemed to be more options.

Musical notes intruded. She hadn't noticed the arrival of another person. An organist, but unlike any organist she had ever imagined. No amateur, and surprisingly a patron of joy, the one element that had been in short supply in her own limited religious experience. A well-dressed man. She assumed this from his back, the only view she had.

She hadn't noticed the arrival of a dozen or more other people, worshippers, welcome every day. She heard murmurings of supplication from bowed heads, fumbling with candles, the quiet hiss of wicks. It wasn't precisely a congregation. It was midweek after all. There was no sermon to be had from the high pulpit. She stayed. She heard the soft-shoed approach of the supplicants, whispered prayers, flicking of umbrellas.

She wondered about the prayers. Were they all requests for intervention from the Almighty to provide what was needed? Words of praise and gratitude? Perhaps not. The murmurings were soft and dour, interspersed with jerking sobs from some. Heads bowed.

Charlotte Bragg lit no candles, offered no supplications, offered no praise. She was not there because she believed that her most cherished desire would come to pass if voiced in this citadel of the holy.

This was the church, the place for the future joyous occasion of a marriage. Tomorrow the building would shudder with joy, with praise. Church bells would ring with celebration. A celebration from which Charlotte has been excluded. She dried tears before they could gain control. Patience learned after a lifetime of caring for others rejected bitterness. Time. She had time.

A wry smile twitched. She should have been sitting in a court. After all, she had been sentenced. A sentence of indefinite duration.

The organ music that flooded every nook and cranny of the vast building was so beautiful that it permeated her whole being. Transfixed, she sat, loath to move away from the sweet, transcendent notes. She didn't know how long she sat, but when the music suddenly stopped, it was as if the air had chilled and been sucked out of the room. She returned to earth with a thud.

She waited until the tingling effect on her body subsided. Then, rubbing the painful hip that she had momentarily forgotten, she rose, gathered her walking cane, and left.

The next day, denied invitation to her elder son's wedding, Charlotte slid into the back pew of the cathedral. A hat of wide proportions hid her from view whenever she chose to conceal her presence. It was a ridiculous hat but there were no odd glances from the one hundred or so guests. The bride, an established actress, had apparently invited every showy person of her acquaintance. Boas, cravats, ruffles and net garments would have fooled the casual observer into assuming that the whole affair was a stage production rather than a wedding.

The flamboyance of the guests on the bride's side of the church was in stark contrast to the austerity of the guests on the groom's side. Black or charcoal suits, slim A line dresses. Chic hats.

From her position in the back corner seat Charlotte saw her two sons arrive. Jack, the groom, yanked at his shirt collar, turned to his grinning brother, Bradley, who gave his brother a reassuring thump and made the sign of the cross—an impertinence that earned him a censorial slap. Squaring his shoulders, Jack turned and stared down the long aisle to the altar.

Large bouquets that festooned the dais were likely the most colourful in the church's 200-year history. All twelve of them.

Bradley Bragg, catching sight of his disobedient parent paled and slid a threatening finger across his throat. Charlotte poked out her tongue. She wasn't leaving until she saw her granddaughter. Bradley had required a promise from their mother to stay away, but she had failed to give more than an ambiguous murmur.

Outside the heavy cathedral doors, three-year-old Jenna Bragg was embroiled in a fiery exchange with Stella, her mother, the bride, who had obviously taken her gown design from a meringue pile-up. The extravagant garment severely impacted her ability to quarrel with her daughter.

Stella attempted to gather the frilly white confection in both hands to better bridge the distance between her and the tiny child. Any delightful anticipation she'd had on leaving home that the child would abandon her usual heathen behaviour and adopt perfect manners for the most auspicious occasion of her mother's life was being dismantled. Jenna Bragg threw a tantrum worthy of a celebrity diva.

Charlotte held the brim of her hat with a gloved hand to hide her face yet still allowed her to observe the war occurring on the church top step. She saw an angelic toddler with blonde curls and a dainty floral headpiece tottering precariously. Jenna stamped her foot.

A slap from the bride, rather than subdue the angel, caused the offended tot to wrench the headpiece from her head, throw it down, then run as fast as her sturdy legs would carry her.

A melee erupted among the five bridesmaids but their efforts to assist were encumbered by tight, oyster-coloured satin dresses that only allowed a paralytic shuffle from the wearer.

Penguin suited ushers hurried to intervene. Jenna had forgotten her purpose for the day and was chasing a one-legged pigeon. On her capture by the boyish usher the tot gave a piercing scream and was brought wriggling and kicking to the frustrated bride. Stella refrained from donating her offspring another slap. Something she would cheerfully have done at any other time and place.

The ruckus attracted the groom to the fray. Jack bent down and soothed the tot, awkwardly placing the headdress back into its original position. He returned quickly to the front of the church.

Jenna, with her head held high in dignified rancour submitted to the clucking of the bridesmaids.

The organ played.

Stella sucked in a shuddering breath.

One of the bridesmaids stroked and soothed the bride's voluminous tulle confection.

'Bridezilla,' muttered Charlotte, momentarily forgetting herself.

The procession began.

Holding a basket of rose petals, Jenna Louise Bragg stomped down the aisle, chucking squashed lumps of red petals at various intervals along the aisle.

It was a sight that would cheer Charlotte Bragg whenever sadness threatened to overwhelm.

*From *Silent Spaces*.

Child thief

I hadn't intended to drag her down, the plump child, sweep her into myself. I want to say that at the outset. It is the fate of all humankind, all life, to return to me, to earth. It wasn't because I loved her more than most, even though I did. Those sweet brown hands that pressed and patted my soil around flowers and plants. Those dimpled hands, tanned by the sun, still plump with childhood.

He had been watching her, the tall corpulent man, with sly eyes that slipped in pout-lipped gaze upon her innocence. I knew what he intended, although the child knew nothing. Nothing other than his wrong-footed gait as he returned from his daily walk. A country stroll, or so it seemed, but no, a purposeful perambulation down shrub-thick eucalypt lined lanes.

At first, in those early walks, he saw nothing, intent on the hidden whiskey bottle in the rutted hollow of a flowering gum. A hollow crumbled from within by gluttonous termite activity. The perfect place for that delight for his drooling lips. Sometimes a sweet Port, away from the probing eyes of his pious wife, the thin Slavic woman. She who denied him every comfort, every act of sympathetic attention.

The thin Slavic woman who ironed his many shirts with rhythmic precision, hiss, slide, thunk, glide, flick, press, turn. He'd seen the act as a tenderness once, in the new days, their soft days, when they both smiled at nothing. When he believed she had the power to cure his dark imaginings, black desires. Now he saw the fussy ironing of his shirts as an indulgent obsession with order, nothing to do with him. Collar, cuffs, yoke, sleeves, press, turn.

She set the table in the same way, straightening knife, fork, spoon; two places. Glass tumbler at the tip of the knife, bread and butter plate, dinner plate, placing them just so. Serving, sitting, then eating quietly, as if he wasn't there.

At night when he rolled onto the thin Slavic woman, as he pumped his seed into her slack body, as if she wasn't there, she wondered which one of them had disappeared first.

He saw nothing on the journey to the dark hollow in the ancient eucalypt even though he flickered pale bloodless eyes, like fluorescent lights, in every direction, until, sure that no one saw, no one knew, he'd guzzle the whiskey from the bottle, sit awhile, sated, but not satisfied, leaning against the gum's rough bark, half-lidded gaze out on the world, first redolent and mellow, before the turning to dark thoughts.

The loud village boys knew his secret lust for the hidden

bottle. But they knew nothing of his other lust, for innocent flesh, for the downy softness of an untouched child. They knew his whiskey trysts, laughed at the futile comedy of his subterfuge, occasionally sipping from the bottle, or spitting in it.

At church the corpulent man sat beside his thin Slavic wife, holding one side of the Hymnal, as she held the other. He came as close to her as he could, without touching.

She sang with gusto, relishing the act of communal praise. It annoyed him, that she could find such gratification, when she gave so little pleasure to him. He didn't sing, there on the lofty balcony that overlooked the lower congregation. He held his head high, posed a thoughtful expression and occasionally mouthed the words.

He was asked on occasion to sit on the rostrum, with the pious, the deacons and the minister. Those men that sometimes called him a model of piety, for driving the truck to help distribute stale bread to the poor, for attending the church working bees and doing his share, and naturally, for his modest but always-witnessed act of placing a bulging tithe envelope in the red velvet offertory bag with scarlet silk lining and lacquered wooden handles, deep pocketed, designed to make gifts to the Lord anonymous.

Sometimes he read a psalm from the high pulpit, with mellifluous voice and correct intonation. A nice baritone, they said, did he want to join the choir? Thanks but no, my work, you see, the travelling, unpredictable. He sang enthusiastically then, on the rostrum behind the pulpit.

Will you read the children's story, down on the carpet at the front of the church? Your voice, so mellow. Not for me, he resisted, there are others are so much better than I.

He dared not come too close to those young agile bodies, sitting cross-legged, heads resting on knees, faces shining in rapt attention, smooth of kin, untouched, ripe. Perhaps an unguarded look, or the licking of lips, might give him away. He dared not.

In the church yard with the other men, wearers of sombre suits, he lamented his childless state with measured grieving. He was sad, but grateful too, for other bounties, health, life, the thin Slavic wife, who volunteered with warmth and cheer, touching the arms of others, gently, with compassion.

The corpulent man passed the yard where she played, the plump child with her solitary games who hummed as she skipped, lilted a song while she tended the small flower bed her father had prepared for her. Like her dead mother, she loved the soil, the smell of earth after rain, the dark richness of loam as she pressed and shaped soft mounds around dahlias, freesias, daisies and trellised sweet peas. She plucked out milk thistles for the chooks, crumbled straw through the soil with patient fingers, running for the hose, looping it across the yard to water, powdering gypsum as her father had shown her, to conquer unyielding clay. Back and forth, pulling the bright yellow wagon her grandmother had bought, with its treasure of miniature gardening tools. Then off to the crooked path to gather the $2 plants, the best her father could afford, rattling and clunking back to the garden bed.

They flourished under her tender touch, the daily ministrations more commonly found in a seasoned nurseryman. A shiny metal watering pot carried water to the more distant plot in the far corner of the yard where she struggled with recalcitrant clumps, batting and thumping with her small spade, until the loamy soil yielded, crumbled, rubbed between small hands to fine breadcrumb texture.

On one such return of the corpulent man, from the whisky bottle in its dank rotting hollow, as mellow thoughts became murky melancholy, he saw her. The plump child, her smooth brown skin, glowing in the sun's midday glory. Behind his lustful eyes, dense shadows reigned. He saw despair everywhere. He saw all he had been denied, success, a laden table. Saw the poverty of his cold, frugal life with the thin Slavic woman whose words and acts were as barren as her ungenerous womb that delivered no sons, no daughters.

He swore. He could not indulge his soaring desire too easily here.

The plump child was adored by her widowed father, as he watched in a different way, fretful at the windows, wanting, needing her safety, her happiness. The widower, a ticket seller at the local rail, worried if the new machines with their faultless technology would replace him. Even there in the village, far from the rush of city commuters with no minutes spare to pass the time of day, with a polite ticket seller intent on wishing them a nice day, answering questions about the inland line, connecting trains, timetables. Could a machine do that? Perhaps he could return to accounting. But that would mean leaving, and could he bear that when the plump child was happy, safe?

She didn't belong in my earth, deep in the soft sweet soil. It was too soon. Too soon for final resting, within my keeping. Dust to dust, earth to earth. But how else could I snatch her from the grasp of the corpulent man, biding his time?

Not today, not with her vigilant father so near.

The corpulent man stumbled and wavered on his way back from the tree, taking pains to appear sober, soughing onto the slatted bench near the park, feigning sleep with a wide brimmed hat concealing watchful eyes as he drank in the fresh laughter and young bodies of the children at play. Little girls in tutus and frills, ribbons and bows, round, ripe torsos and agile limbs as they cartwheeled, slid and squealed.

He only surrendered to forbidden fruit, the bloodlust for innocence on his rare trips to the city, where playgrounds were vast domains near thick bushland, unfenced. There he carefully sought and selected his prey. The petite blonde, shy and patient, waiting for the slide, taking her turn in the queue, allowing others to push her aside. Do you like my puppy? I've lost his lead, will you help me find it? My eyes, not so good, you see. How kind you are. How bright, how fresh. We haven't come far, there's the park, you see it? Is that it? Don't cry, don't scream.

Thrust clothing aside, pink tutu, purple leggings, belt buckle fumbling, grasping, taking—release, hard-breath panting. Concealment in the hessian bag he'd left there hours before. Crushing heel on the puppy. A patient man, the corpulent man, prepared.

The fire in his veins was growing stronger, searing. It was only a matter of time before he would plunder and violate again. This time closer to home. His thick fat hands covering soft mouths to silence screams as he roamed and plundered. Grip the throat, shake out the light, then toss aside a ragdoll child, lifeless, spent, destined for burial in my earth. Too young, too soft, too soon.

That's why I took her, before he could.

The rains came. I rumbled and spilled a mountain of soil, over him, over her, as he approached, reached with death-lust eyes.

A random mudslide, they said, a freakish thing for this part of the country, unfathomable. A heavy summer downpour. A torrent that swept them both away, away from the garden, away from the fretful widower, away from the thin Slavic woman, the pious Sunday men.

She was already unconscious, the plump child, hit by a flailing rock from the garden border, caught in the deluge, as the flowers she nurtured, still too tender, were swept away with her, far from the corpulent man who had his own journey to take, his own destination.

He gargled and sputtered on silty flood waters, struggling a tide he didn't foresee. He hadn't heard the rumble of muddy slime, the swift crack of thunder. All had faded with the buzzing in his ears of his own lust, rushing through his veins, dulling his senses.

The corpulent man, the child thief, smelled fear then, his own. Fear tightened his throat as the floodwaters shook and tumbled him, stealing his breath. Branches tumbled and bruised, tore and rent his dying flesh. He tasted the iron of his own blood. A foot snagged on a submerged log. He sunk, eyes bulging, into the deep, limp, lifeless.

The log shifted under the force of the waters, freeing his corpse, tossing him ashore like a ragdoll with the flood detritus where the stream fanned out to the sea.

They found him there, bloated and blue, preyed on by crabs and crows, partly concealed by muddy sticks and leaves. No one had heard his screams, his strangled cries for help.

The child was in my loving embrace, earthen, in the soil she loved. Too soon.

The fretful widower saw her red-shoed foot. He battled with my clutch of her, his hands digging, gouging the mud, scooping it aside, bailing it away like water in a sinking boat, dragging aside mud and sticks until he found her soft limp mouth, shook the silt from its cavern and breathed air between blue lips, until she retched and spewed.

They heard his cries as he struggled to remove the mud that sucked at her lower body, imprisoning her. They came, fought, and carried her home.

The bottle washed up near the corpulent man, rocking with the tide against his swollen body, taunting, empty of its numbing delirium.

The thin Slavic woman, the wife of the corpulent man, set the table precisely, two places, cutlery lined to perfection, a glass tumbler on the right side of the dinner plate near the tip of the knife, then she sat, eating quietly. He wasn't there.

Reality suspended ...

The books had sat side by side for so long that no one noticed what had happened, least of all the housekeeper, Mrs Campberwell, whose duty it was to clean and maintain her master's library. That dreary obligation had been neglected of late, due to Lord Dainsbury's propensity to confine himself to the warmer rooms in the North Wing.

This circumstance led to Mrs Campberwell taking the liberty of ignoring the library altogether, which was just as well because that august woman would never have taken the strain of realising that two of his Lordship's First Edition hardcover classics had, in fact, become one volume.

Stranger things happened as many of the books combined, releasing the characters into the room, although dusty and neglected was still an elegant room with magnificent furniture and décor. A situation much appreciated by Mrs Scarlett Butler. Throwing off her initial shock and confusion at her mysterious conveyance to another place, her resourcefulness came to the fore. She perceived the superiority of her new surroundings to her beloved estate of Tara, in every regard other than pure sentiment. Upon finding herself in a new establishment, she decided to make the best of things. Settling in an elegant crimson chaise longue with her green ball gown draped to show her figure to its best advantage she looked around the room. The books trembled.

In a far corner of the room, Mr. Fitzwilliam Darcy was engaged in a tense conversation with Miss Elizabeth Bennet. Scarlett coughed loudly. The pair ignored her presence. There was something almost lover-like about their exchange and yet they appeared to be at odds. When Miss Bennet stepped back angrily Scarlett rose quietly and crossed the room. This Mr Darcy was a handsome devil. Fluttering her fan, she flirted with him outrageously.

Even though Mr Darcy appeared to be a man of few words, things were progressing beautifully until the arrival of Rhett Butler. Scarlett was elated, but rather than pay attention to his wilful wife, Rhett became entranced by the wit and charm of Miss Bennet. Scarlett stamped her foot. She would not be bested by a country miss, English rose or no. The books shook.

When Heathcliff slipped into the picture with his brooding intensity and careless ways Scarlett was diverted. Now here was a man to match her. She had just caught his attention when the voice of a child intruded. It was a Miss Mary Lennox seeking Misselthwaite Manor. Her arrival was closely followed by Huckleberry Finn and the slave Jim who was instantly mistaken for Othello.

A dense noise erupted. The authors of those famous works arrived and began to argue loudly. The library shelves begin to shake as the books battled to combine. The ruckus attracted Mrs Campberwell, who fell in a dead faint upon opening the library door.

The book guardian

Ephram Garibaldi pressed a rheumy finger on the panel at the back wall of the library. He watched the glass doors glide shut, while the security shutters rolled smoothly down, cutting out the twilight.

'Silent as the grave, young Mark,' he said.

'At least white noise has been eliminated in this new world.' Mark tapped his foot.

'You say that like it's a good thing.'

'Well, isn't it? I mean...'

'Ah, young Mark, if only you had seen the world I lived in. Leaves fluttering down, birdsong.'

'Ah music.' Mark reached for the electronic panel.

'No. Not that manufactured e-streaming stuff.' Ephram waved a dismissive arm. 'The real thing.'

'Sorry.' Mark let his arm drop.

'It's okay, Mark. I'm not upset with you. And I won't go on about how things once were. You've heard enough of my ranting about the things we lost in the Third Age of Technology.' Ephram sighed. 'It was bad enough losing the natural world, but now they are pressuring everyone to buy tickets to the Palindrome in the Ancient Natural Order Museum to see a "3D experience of the past in living visual and sound"! Pfft, *living*, it's an insult! A theatrical production is a poor replacement for what we had before humanity destroyed nature.'

Mark rocked on his feet, his eyes alight. 'But we have the books, you saved them. Well, some of them anyway.'

'Shh, young Mark. We don't discuss this here remember.' Ephram put a hand on the boy's shoulder. 'What a wonderful thing it is that I found you. You're a wonderful help,' he said, eyeing the surveillance cameras. 'Well, it's time to leave.'

Mark smiled and winked. Ephram frowned. The boy really must learn to be more careful in the library. Every movement and sound was recorded. The consequences were unthinkable. All those years of reclaiming books would be undone. As it was, he'd only saved one copy of each book and sent the rest to the relevant Transformation Centres. He didn't dare take more. It was hard enough to hide them in the early days, and it was getting harder.

Ephram took the small disc that locked the room, tapping it as he ushered Mark out the side door of the library and headed to the lifts. Mark flicked furtive looks down the corridor and Ephram rolled his eyes. The boy was so obvious. He waited until the lift doors had closed before pressing B for the lower floor instead of M for the main entrance level. Their subterfuge must not be detected.

'I found a student trying to download more data than his quota today,' Mark said. 'Don't they realise every byte is detected the minute it's accessed? There are signs up everywhere. Then there was one girl who had two storage units on her arm and tried to get double by using different access points. She'd borrowed her boyfriend's Xephar, she thought he had reconfigured it to her ID code, but our systems are too good for that. There's a penalty, so I deactivated her Xephar for three months.'

'Was she the one with the bright pink Xephar?'

'Yeah, pretty cool.'

'I don't know why anyone wants coloured ones. I still haven't got used to those things. It's crazy to think they've invented a device that is magnetised to bone. They look like bandaids.'

'What are bandaids?' asked Mark.

'Well, they were ... Never mind, go on with your story.'

While paying scant attention to Mark's nervous chatter, Ephram allowed his thoughts to wander. How he'd scoffed when people predicted books would be obsolete one day. What a fool he'd been. He'd made an application to DAFTU the Data Antiquities & Securities Technology Union for the Canberra Library & Data Bureau to become the central site for sorting and processing books.

That had been Ephram's first win. All the books came to him for collation. He put the earliest edition aside. Then he selected a good edition of each book and carefully wrapped it for the courier to take it to the Commonwealth Ancient Arts Museum & Gallery. The rest went in the boxes and were labelled RECONCEIVING before being sent on. When he had tried to access the online data for the reconceiving process, he'd found nothing. Not even the usual overblown government propaganda. Nothing. If only he knew what was happening to the books. What did reconceiving mean? He hated the word.

The lift door slid open. They entered the basement. It was a cold dark labyrinth with a dank odour. Mark was silent as they walked past the storage units for broken technology and outdated tablets. These units were only accessed twice a year when the equipment was sorted.

There were so many unused storage areas due to outsourcing of the cleaning and maintenance work that Ephram had had his pick of rooms thirty years ago. Not much had changed down here since then. No one came if they could avoid the place.

'We can't stay long tonight,' said Mark.

'I know,' said Ephram, 'there have been cuts to the number of Xubers. Where would we be without those driverless, soulless transport modules?' He pictured the sleek half-moon-shaped vehicles that glided around the city in their grooved tracks.

'Yes, they only come every hour now, but they do take you to your own door.' Mark shrugged. 'I've never known anything else. I guess it was different for you.'

'Yes. There was a strange satisfaction in having a steering wheel in your hands, deciding your own destination, even changing your mind if you felt like it. Stopping off at the grocery store.'

'Grocery store?'

'Before your time, boy. Food and nutrition lists weren't

always collated from an electronic setting on the pantry and fridge, beeped in and out and then delivered.'

'Wow, I wondered where food came from. Cool.'

Ephram sighed. He pulled out an ancient key and opened a dark grey door. Most of the storage rooms had been updated to electronic entry, but there were a few that had been overlooked, and this room was the largest of those with keyed entry. Ephram had overheard one of the retrieval maintenance men ask, 'What kind of technology opens those doors with the funny holes?' Ephram had smiled. The room would be left alone.

Mark set his Xephar alarm. Their time was limited. Thirty short minutes. They sat in silence with their chosen books from the shelves.

Ephram caressed the leather binding of 1984, a limited edition, much like the one he had hidden at home in the apartment he had shared with Evelyn before she died, and now Bluebell. At least he still qualified to have a cat. What pets would replace cats in the evolution of technological living? Cockroaches? He chuckled.

'Can't get into it, Ephram?' said Mark, pointing at his companion's unopened book.

'No, must be showing my age.'

'It's great they let you work over 85 isn't it?'

'Used to think so, boy.'

The Xephar alarm sounded.

Carefully replacing the books the two men left.

It was chilly at the Xuber exchange. They greeted two men who were also waiting. One wore a suit and a pin on his lapel that showed he worked for the government. The other wore casual clothes and had a large box on a trolley.

'Bit small,' said the suited man, eyeing the box.

'They're flatpacked,' the other man responded. He turned to Ephram. 'When is the next Xuber to the city?' Ephram looked at his Xephar, but Mark was quicker and already had the correct screen up.

'You might have trouble putting that thing in the Xuber,' said Mark. 'What is it anyway?'

'Mark!' Ephram frowned. 'Sorry, the impudence of the young.'

'It doesn't matter,' said the man. He looked at the suited man for approval. The suit shrugged. 'We're launching these on the international news tonight. I'm the artist who's designed them. It's so exciting. We've been working on these for years, using all the recycled books.'

'The books?' Ephram paled.

'Yes. I have a prototype sculpture in here. There were so many proposal ideas, but this was Senator Citrine's brainchild.' The artist gestured towards the suited man who smiled in the deferential manner of the supremely vain. 'I just executed the idea. I had to conduct a lot of research. These are magnificent, if I do say myself. Senator Citrine has been assisting with the funding. Actually, it's all down to him really. Right from the concept that paper books were an unacceptable drain on the environment.'

'Really,' said Ephram, turning to the politician. 'Senator Citrine. The man of the hour. Humph.'

Ephram looked at the box. 'Where will these, um, sculptures be displayed?'

'Well, naturally they will only be placed in areas of top security,' said the Senator.

'Like Parliament House?' Ephram glared.

'Well, yes and a few select residences.'

'Yes.' The artist leaned forward. 'It's exciting. Naturally the Senator has one. Along with his environmental award.'

The senator waved a dismissive hand, a gesture to affirm his humility for such a high honour.

'Amazing,' said Ephram, teeth clenched. He stood in front of the senator. 'May I ask what the books have been reconceived as?'

'Ubertrees.' The man smiled widely.

'Uber *what*?' Ephram's voice was a tense squeak.

'Trees.'

Ephram snapped. His fist connected with the Senator's jaw.

'Not bad for eighty-eight,' he said as Mark dragged him away.

Travails of a time traveller's assistant

Wesley stood outside the office of Goodwin Investigations & Recovery Agency. It was an old stone building in an upmarket area of the city. He was early for an interview as personal assistant. The Goodwin Agency was prestigious. The hours were flexible and the pay rate was more than generous. He loved being an artist, but even though his paintings sold well, the money was irregular.

Taking a moment to check his appearance in the large glass windows, he realised he should have had a haircut. He put a hand up to tidy his hair and saw a daub of paint on his hand. So much for a good first impression.

While the Estefans' Café & Restaurant opposite was enjoying brisk trade, there was no-one on the Agency side of the street. Wesley wondered how many other applicants would be attending. Squaring his shoulders, he pushed open the ancient timber and glass door. A bell tinkled in the back room. He looked around. The office resembled something out of the Forties with its antique furniture.

A tall, elegant woman was shuffling papers on a mahogany desk that dominated the room. 'Drat,' she said, as a sheaf of papers hit the ground and slid across the floor.

Wesley stooped to retrieve them.

'Don't worry, young man. I'll do it later. I need to pick them up in a particular order.' The woman tucked a stray strand of coal black hair into an off-kilter bun that was held in place with a pencil. 'I'm Veronica Goodwin, owner, investigator, dogsbody, you name it. And you are Wesley Brent.' She twisted around, eyes scanning the room. 'Now where are those ... darn, can't find a thing. Nice to meet you.' With a distracted smile she reached out and shook his hand. 'Well, Wesley Brent, you can see my drastic need for a personal assistant. She gestured at the shambles of paperwork on her desk. 'Please take a seat.'

Wesley folded his lanky frame onto the chair. He opened his mouth to begin the spiel he'd been rehearsing for days, but Veronica had flipped open the laptop and was tapping random keys.

'Wretched thing. I hope you understand it,' she said. The computer beeped into life. Veronica squeaked in surprise. She shuffled the papers on her desk. 'Oh, there they are,' she said, placing a dark rimmed pair of glasses on her face with a satisfied sigh. 'I hope you'll like it here, Wesley. The job is yours.'

'Oh? I thought this was an interview. The employment agency told me to bring these.' Wesley held up a black folder.

'Daft lot, those agency people. I have all your

information on file.'

Wesley's eyebrows flew up. 'You do?'

'Naturally. Um, cyberspace, internet, you know.' She pointed at the computer, eyeing it suspiciously.

'Ah, the agency sent my information. I see.'

Veronica frowned, then seemed relieved. 'Ah yes, that must be it.' The computer pinged. Veronica shut the lid down. 'I see you're quite the artist.'

'How did you know that?' Wesley squirmed in the chair.

'I've seen you painting the mural for the Estefans' café opposite.'

'Oh, of course.'

Veronica leaned back. 'I believe you are perfect for the job Wesley. You have a good reputation for confidentiality.'

'But I haven't worked as a personal assistant before.'

'You're much too humble Wesley Brent. Always have been. Why that fiasco back at University, with the student newspaper—you only wanted to protect Sara, of course, sorting the petty cash theft by replacing the money yourself. Wouldn't have worked the second time though.'

'Say again.' Wesley sat bolt upright. 'How can you possibly ...?'

Wesley mopped his forehead with a handkerchief that had seen better days.

'Oh Wesley, the world is never quite what it seems.' Veronica smiled. 'I'll start from the beginning...'

Wesley slumped in the chair.

Veronica brought him a glass of water. 'I'm a time traveller Wesley, you know—travelling to different...'

Wesley choked on a sip of water. When the coughing fit ceased, he viewed the woman opposite him with watery eyes and a shocked expression.

'Oh dear. You look like you want to run out the door. Please stay and hear me out, Wesley.'

'Don't think I could stand if I tried.'

'I'll give you time to take it all in. I can almost see the cogs in your head turning. You were like that back then too.'

'So, you *were* there. I don't remember seeing you. Were you invisible?'

Veronica laughed. 'One Superpower at a time please!'

'Wait a minute—you said something about the *second* time. There wasn't a second theft.'

'Ah Wesley, but there so very nearly was.'

Wesley leaned forward, alert. 'Ah. I know. A week after the money went missing I was working late on the artwork for the paper. There was an almighty noise, but there was nothing out of place. I would've searched longer but Sara phoned me from the hospital. Her father had broken his leg.'

Regret flashed across Veronica's face. 'Were you alone in the building, Wesley?'

'Well yes. Everyone had gone home. Wait on, there was just a janitor, some new woman. Said she hadn't seen anything, kept her head down. Funny sort of a ... Oh my god, *that was you*!'

Veronica nodded. 'There was a reason you were protecting Sara. Apart from the massive crush you had on her. You thought she knew something.'

Wesley flushed.

'Oh, you poor dear. You're still carrying a flame for the girl. After ten years. It was a noble thing to do—replacing the money. Ill advised, but noble.'

'Sara was the only other one with the keys to the office. But I knew it wasn't her.'

'And you were right. She didn't. It was her father.'

Wesley's face turned white. 'Her father? *Bill took it!*'

The phone jangled. Veronica picked it up, and in perfect diction spoke into the mouthpiece. 'You have reached the office of Goodwin Investigations & Recovery Agency. This is an automated message. We apologise for not being available, but your call is important to us. Please leave a message and we will return your call.'

Wesley's mouth dropped open. 'You're good, you think quickly. Guess you've been doing that for centuries.' He held up a hand. 'Don't tell me. I don't want to know. But, how did Bill take the money?'

'Simple really. Crime often is. He only had to stay hidden in the staff toilets in the main administration block at closing time, then slip out the fire exit afterwards. Security wasn't great in those days, as you'll remember. He was disappointed to find less than $50 the first time so he decided to make another attempt.'

'Oh dear, this is starting to make sense. Bill was always short of cash. He would borrow from Sara. I'm pretty sure he had a gambling problem. But I never thought he'd do something like that. Sara can't possibly know. It would break her heart.' Wesley ran tense fingers through his hair.

'I was just returning from the toilets when I heard the ruckus. What on earth did you do to stop him?'

'Simple. I came rattling past with the cleaning trolley. Bill got a shock, lost his balance, then ran off.'

'But his broken leg?' Wesley rested his elbows on the desk, watching Veronica intently.

'Bill's, er, shall we say "loan officer", was waiting for the money in the car park with a couple of thugs.'

'Bill said he'd stopped to help a homeless man and been attacked. My God, the lies he told.'

'That man was trouble. I think that's why Sara has that bad boy attraction thing going on. It's often the way. It's why nice guys like you finish last.'

'Just for once I'd like to finish first, with Sara. Do you think...'

A loud knock at the door deferred any words of wisdom Veronica may have offered. It was Estella Estefan with two pizza boxes. The aroma filled the room. Wesley's stomach growled.

'Estella, how kind,' said Wesley, ushering the woman inside with a grin, 'but where is Veronica's pizza? She'll be hungry too.'

Estella slapped his arm. 'You tease an old woman too much, Wesley. One is for your new boss. You have the job? Yes?'

Veronica nodded and laughed.

'Good,' said Estella. 'Don't you be letting this one have your pizza, Senora. Like a horse he eats and yet he stays thin and handsome. It's enough to make a woman cry.'

After they had eaten, Veronica became crisp and businesslike, filling Wesley in on his duties. She flitted around the room, clouding the air with exotic perfume as she detailed his role and explained the filing system and client records.

Wesley's eyes widened when Veronica told him that her previous assistant, Evan, was still back in time. 'He's lost, somewhere,' she said, quickly wiping a tear aside. 'So you see, you really must be very particular.'

Veronica handed Wesley a handwritten list.

Stay close.
Follow instructions immediately without question.
Don't act on any other matter except the case in hand.
Don't interact with anyone you know unless it's unavoidable.
If you speak to anyone, say nothing to affect their destiny.

Worry lines creased Wesley's forehead as he contemplated the last line. He held it up. 'I hope you don't expect me to eat this list Veronica, if that's what is needed, because I don't think I could fit it in after all that pizza.'

'You've been watching too many movies.' Veronica laughed. 'And they said you were boring.'

'Who said that?' Wesley shrugged. 'Never mind, I don't want to know.'

'Precisely why I hired you, Wesley Brent. Tomorrow we begin...'

As soon as Wesley walked through the door the next morning he saw Veronica buzzing around the room. She retrieved a small card from the file with a photograph attached.

'This one will do today, Wesley.' She tapped the client card with a red nailed finger. 'Are you ready?'

The first mission wasn't what he had anticipated. He'd expected to be involved in preventing some terrible event in history—a bombing or a plane crash at the very least. But that first assignment had been a tense waiting game in a seedy downtown bar, late on a wintry night a mere ten years in the past.

A middle aged socialite had paid an exorbitant fee for Veronica to intercept her husband, an ageing Don Juan, from meeting his current mistress. Because the wife had no way of knowing the exact moment her husband had met the dazzling creature who'd become his latest lover, Veronica and Wesley endured a long wait.

The prospective mistress was in an upstairs room singing a collection of sultry ballads. The cheating husband didn't arrive for hours. Finally, he swept through the door bringing an icy blast.

Veronica flicked a cigarette lighter near the fire sensor. A narrow flame rose and flickered unnoticed. The alarm shrieked. Chaos reigned. Patrons screamed and shoved, desperate to escape. Wesley seized the man's arm and ushered him into a waiting taxi. The would-be lover was on his way in a matter of minutes, none the wiser.

Over the next few months Veronica relaxed. Wesley was

sure she had grown to trust him. She didn't comment any further about Evan. Perhaps he had failed to stay near her when they were on a mission or broken one of the other rules.

They slipped into an easy routine. Veronica gave him a brief outline of the mission ahead along with concise instructions. Then they entered the creaky lift at the rear of the building; their conduit to another time. Veronica used an ornate fob watch to select the parameters of their destination. When they stepped out of the lift they were at the precise location and time she had programmed.

It was Wesley's job to arrange incidentals. Detours and meals were often necessary and it was also his role to source the correct money and maps. Wesley hadn't imagined these necessities, but it made sense that even supernatural powers needed organisation. Once they were on assignment, Veronica had bigger things to worry about.

When the mission was complete, Veronica signalled to Wesley. Taking the small black mobile he'd been given, he pressed *. That summoned the lumbering George with their taxi. The taxi was different according to the era, but it was always George who collected them. When they were in the taxi Veronica tapped the watch. They were instantly back in the lift at the office.

To Wesley's disappointment, the assignments continued to be mundane. They stopped Mrs Damson's Labrador wandering from home. They travelled back to the day Mrs Wiltshire decided to dye her hair a fiery red. One assignment had involved showing up at a ritzy hotel to remind a young bride-to-be to pick up her handbag containing a ridiculously expensive engagement ring. They sent Mrs Beverley home early from the supermarket the day the decorators were due, forestalling a 'truly hideous colour choice' by her husband who was taking revenge on his wife for inviting her mother to stay.

Wesley consoled himself with the thought that his new life was the closest he'd ever come to being a hero. Anyway, he had plenty to keep him busy. There was research in the library to ascertain whether the client was attempting to use their services for criminal purposes. 'Better safe than sorry,' Veronica said. And there was always the weather to check.

Winter slipped into spring. Wesley finished painting the mural for the Estefan's and had arranged to meet Sara at the café after work. The mural was a vibrant portrayal of life in Italy. Wesley had painted all the Estefan family members from their village, sitting at tables and dancing in the square.

The last rays of the sun slanted onto the rooftops. Wesley whistled as he walked. He was looking forward to spending the evening with Sara. The café was their favourite eatery. It was full of the aromas of Italy and throbbed with the hum of friendship and life. Inside, the stucco walls were painted a muted crimson. The floor was covered with black and white harlequin tiles that shone and sparkled all day. Estella achieved this by rolling out an ancient metal bucket and mop at least half a dozen times a day.

Wesley greeted them and sat with Dimitri.

'Oi, that woman, she makes me tired,' Dimitri said. 'She will wash away the tiles and we will have just concrete left.'

Estella swished the mop in the direction of her husband. 'Why are you sitting old man?' she asked. The men exchanged sly looks and grinned. 'Oh, you have finish our mural Wesley? May I see? Dimitri does not let me have even one peek.'

'Come woman, and stop your bellyaching at me.' Dimitri led the way outside.

Estella wiped her apron across watery eyes. 'Bellissimo Wesley! Where did you learn such things? It is just like home.' Her voice was rich and caressing. She embraced Wesley. 'Why did you not wait for Sara? Oh see, here she is now.'

Wesley turned. Sara had left her corporate image behind. Her long chestnut hair was loose and she wore a casual sundress. She looked like sunshine, young and free. The image of her in the twilight reminded him of the first time he'd seen her at their University orientation event. He found it hard to breathe and hoped she didn't notice.

Estella bounded to meet Sara and swept her aside. 'Ciao bella. Is not the mural Wesley painted bellisimo? He is wonderful. And so are you, coming to help an old man with his accounts. Grazie, molte grazie.'

Estella cleared the tables while Wesley swept the floor.

Dimitri sat at the corner table with Sara. He leant over the old ledger stained with sauces from the kitchen. The old man watched the earnest young woman tally the accounts; her eyes alight with enthusiasm.

'How can you love numbers on a page?' Dimitri said, 'when there is so much more.' He placed his hand on his heart.

Sara looked up. 'Are you all right, Dimitri?'

'Of course, cara. It is *your* heart I think about. It is for you time to fall in love.'

Sara laughed. 'I have had too much love, Dimitri.'

'You have had too much something, I think. But it is not too much love.'

'I keep getting love wrong, Dimitri.'

'It's not the love you get wrong cara, I think you maybe get the wrong man.' Dimitri removed his glasses and wiped them on his red handkerchief. 'Don't listen to me. I'm just an old man who wishes everyone happy.' He glanced across at Wesley who was emptying bins while Estella sang to the pigeons crooning on the beams under the awnings. 'Come, enough work. Wesley, join us and celebrate.'

Dimitri brought two bottles of red wine, dragging Estella from her cleaning on the way.

As the chill of the evening fell, Estella lit the candles and coaxed Dimitri to dance with her.

Wesley took Sara's hands and led her to a space between the tables. He pulled her close. 'This will have to be a very slow dance Sara, there is not much room.'

'The mural is wonderful, Wesley,' said Sara. 'I don't know how you've had time for it. You've been helping me set up my new office on top of your own work. It's a big step for me, starting an accountancy practice on my own. I couldn't have done it without you, you know. You're my best friend.' She gave a nervous laugh. 'I don't know how you've put up with me. All those tears I've cried on your shoulder over some stupid man.'

Wesley struggled to find words, but couldn't. Instead, he kissed the top of her head. *Just one tear for me, Sara. I'd give anything for you to cry one tear for me,* he thought.

Sara put down her glass and took Wesley's hand. 'I have something I want to ask you.'

Wesley's eyes searched hers.

'I would really like you to be my partner in the business. We're a great team.'

Disappointment formed a lump in Wesley's throat. 'I'm sorry, Sara. I have a job,' he said, his voice thin. 'It's, well it's important. I help Veronica find things and people, make a difference.' He spun her around, forcing a smile and cursing his cowardice for not revealing the real reason— that it would be unbearable to see her all the time, loving her as he did. Friendship would have to do.

'I'm sorry. I shouldn't have asked,' she said.

He blanched at the pain in her eyes. He smiled to soften the words. They continued to dance, but the mood between them had changed. Estella chided the grandchildren for peeking when they should have been in bed. Wesley heard the deep rumble of Dimitri's words of love to his wife and her laughing response. He experienced a sharp pang of longing and drew Sara closer.

The next morning Wesley woke early and ran a hasty hand through his hair. His mind was annoyingly foggy. He must have had too much red wine. It had been a magical evening. While Sara was in his arms he had almost hoped ... but now he had to focus on the day and the next mission. When he arrived at the office Veronica briefed him. Derby Day,

Kentucky, 1974. A father had gambled away his daughter's college fund on a 20-1 horse named Patience.

At the races they recognised their target from the photo his daughter had provided. The man was waiting for the betting booth to open. He paced, patting a fat wallet. Veronica tipped a glass of wine on him and began a long-winded argument with him. He missed the queue.

'That's great,' said Wesley. 'All over quickly.'

'I wish it was that simple. There are three more days of the racing carnival.'

'Oh. He's still going to blow his money, isn't he?'

Veronica sighed. 'If he gets the chance. We'll have to stay. Tramping around a soggy racetrack isn't my idea of fun but we must see this through.'

Wesley wondered if Veronica ever tired of time travel. Being a Superhero wasn't all it was cracked up to be as far as he could see. He booked them into a small Bed & Breakfast near the racecourse.

Their man was a vain and superficial creature who seemed to care only for fancy clothes, inane conversation and copious quantities of whisky, and survived on a few hours' sleep at night. Wesley could quietly murder him. God only knows what *that* would do to the cosmos. Veronica was in fine form. She managed to prevent the man from placing a single bet. After the final race was run, the two time travellers sat exhausted in the refreshments marquee.

'The last three days have been the most terminally boring of my entire life,' said Wesley, resting his head on the back of the chair.

Veronica dropped her wine glass. Wesley put a hand on her arm. 'Veronica! You're as white as a ghost!'

Veronica's hands shook. Her eyes were fixed on some point in the straggling crowd that was streaming towards the exit gates. All at once she was off, throwing herself into the jubilant arms of a well-built man with a thatch of blonde hair. Spinning her around, the man rained kisses on her neck.

Wesley froze.

'What the...? Veronica! You'll mess with the time space continuum thingy.'

Veronica turned to face him, her arm firmly around the man beside her. 'It's all right, Wesley.'

'No it's not! This can't be good, it's dangerous. It's against the rules—*your* rules.' He reached for his notebook. It wasn't in his pocket. 'This can't be happening. We'll never get home.'

'Wesley, stop. This is ... my assistant, the one I lost, remember?'

Wesley gaped at them. 'Evan?'

'Yes, Evan. Evan *Goodwin*.' Veronica placed a gloved hand on Wesley's arm. 'Everything is as it should be, Wesley.' She peeled the glove from her hand, revealing a wedding ring. 'This is where I belong. Here with Evan; in the past.'

'Oh! I see,' he said, scratching his head. 'Actually, I don't see at all.'

Veronica smiled a soft smile of regret. 'Think about it, dear man.'

'Oh, my! So, I'm from the future.'

'Yes, Wesley dear.'

It was quiet in the taxi with George. Wesley watched the outside world blur by the darkened taxi window.

'What happens now, George?'

'Whatever you choose, Wesley.' George handed him the fob watch; the key to going home.

Wesley looked down at the watch. The legacy of time travel was now his to accept or reject. He could be the next Superhero if he wished.

Wesley handed the watch back. 'You tap it George. I'm going home. For Good.'

He ran from the lift. The office didn't even warrant a sideways glance. He needed Sara, wanted her. He would accept the partnership. She might come to love him. It was worth the chance.

Sara stared out into the darkness. The city lights blinked mutely. Where on earth was Wesley? He'd been gone for days. She wound her hair around tense fingers, wavering between anxiety about his safety and anger that he hadn't called. Now and then, she wiped salty wetness from her face.

She thought of everything they'd been through together. All the times he had been her calm and stable rock. She thought of the weeks she had spent with him after his parents died, when he hadn't been able to face the world. She'd made him get up and keep going, forced him to eat, gone through every corner of the cottage he grew up in, sorting all the possessions of his parents' lives. She remembered all the times they'd helped each other shift. When had her feelings turned to love? How had she ever been content with friendship with this wonderful man? The one who never let her down. She wept bitter tears. Tears for Wesley.

Finally, as the pink dust of dawn intruded, she curled into a ball on the sofa and fell asleep.

There was a loud rap on the door.

She flung it open.

'Sara, you really must remember to check who's at the door before you ... Oh no, you've been crying.'

She crushed him to her.

'Who hurt you this time?' Wesley murmured against her ear. 'I'll kill him.'

'Then you will have to kill yourself, you idiot! Where have you been? I've been worried out of my mind!' She rained salty kisses on him.

'I haven't been gone that long,' he said. 'What do you mean? I'm the one who hurt you?'

'Do I have to spell it out for you Wesley?' Sara's eyes sparkled.

'Yes, please.' Wesley drew her closer and manoeuvred them to the couch where he pulled her into his lap. 'Spelling would be great. I've always liked spelling. Did I tell you I won a spelling bee once...'

Sara silenced him with a lingering kiss.

'I think you misspelled that. You may have to do it

again.'

Sara laughed. 'I love you.'

'It's about time. I've loved you for ages.' Wesley smiled. 'Now *do* stop interrupting a perfectly good spelling lesson.' He returned her kisses with all the passion of those hungry years.

The loud clock

Georgia dragged her feet as she watched her brother's long strides swirl dust on the bush track ahead. It was alright for him. He wanted to go. Lifting her long, tangled hair, she shifted her backpack to her left shoulder. She wished she'd had time to tie her hair up, but Mark had been impatient to leave.

At sixteen, he was four years older than Georgia, and already taller than their father. Georgia was tiny and as lively as a hummingird. She stopped to watch a white-naped honeyeater tease nectar from a wattle flower with its brush-tipped tongue. Georgia loved birds. She hoped to see the barn owl at Tina's.

'It's an Australian masked owl or *Tyto novaehollandiae,*' Tina had announced proudly at school. 'It's called a masked owl because of its white, heart-shaped face.' She'd done an elaborate project with her father.

'Hurry up, Squib,' called Mark. 'We're nearly there. Don't ya even wanna come?'

'Not that you care.'

'What'd ya say?'

'I'll get there. Look, you go. I won't tell Mum and Dad I walked the last bit on my own.'

Mark took off at a run with his backpack thumping.

Georgia sighed, wondering why she'd agreed to come. It wasn't as if she and Tina were friends. Their parents were friends. Their brothers were friends. But she and Tina were just ... unlikely, both twelve, but sharing little else. Hardly enough for a weekend. In the grey concrete world of their small-town school, Georgia went about rushing, soothing, motor-mouthing. Tina, with her slow, sly winks at the boys, taunted and bullied Georgia.

The thing was, it was easier to be Tina's friend than not. It was different for Georgia's brother Mark. He'd been looking forward to the visit for weeks. Tina's brother, Kyle, was his best friend.

The house was built lengthways on the narrow block. Thick, untamed Grevilleas hemmed it in. The entrance was at the side, down a gravel driveway. The curtains were closed, leaving the front room dark and musty. The windows were shut to keep out draughts. The rooms were airless.

Tina waved Georgia inside. 'Shut the door. And take off your shoes. I thought you'd be here earlier to help me with tea.'

'Where's your mum?' Georgia tripped on the uneven floors as she followed Tina to the kitchen-cum-dining-room at the back of the house.

'In bed, sick, as usual.' Tina wore a faded, sunflower-patterned apron and carried a paring knife. 'Here,' she said, handing it to Georgia, 'you can cut the onions.'

'Onions?'

'Yeah. Seen one before?' Tina handed Georgia a wooden board grooved by years of cutting and slicing. After watching Georgia's inept attempts, Tina brushed her aside and handed her a potato peeler and a bowl instead.

'Do you like our clock?' asked Tina, pointing at a tall Grandfather clock that jutted out and divided the dining area from the kitchen. 'It's antique. It's worth heaps of money.'

'It's ... it has nice wood,' said Georgia, biting her lip. She bent to pick up an errant slice of potato peel.

'You're not very good at helping, are you Georgia?' Tina took the bowl of potatoes, checked them for remaining skin, rinsed then sliced them with angry stabs, before plopping them into a boiling pot.

Tina's mother arrived for dinner in her dressing gown, a ragged garment that might once have been green or grey. She ate listlessly and didn't contribute to the conversation which was left mainly to Tina and her father. The boys had little to say. As soon as the meal was over, the adults disappeared.

'Where is everyone?' asked Georgia.

Tina rolled her eyes. 'It's just us. We clean up.'

'Don't worry, Squib. We'll help, won't we Kyle?' Mark winked at Tina and picked up a tea towel.

Kyle moved close to Georgia, slant-eyed, smiling slowly. She froze. His eyes spoke an unknown language as his tongue rolled around his lips. Startled, she looked to Mark, but he and Tina were laughing and flicking tea towels at each other. Kyle moved closer, pressing her with his lean body.

Georgia tried to breathe, but her throat cramped. Soon she was hard up against the unflinching weight of the Grandfather clock. It grew louder, *tuck, tuck*. And still he pushed, *tuck, tuck*. He sloped a smile and walked away, casually joining the conversation of the others. He turned and made a primal gesture at her.

Georgia mutely followed Tina's instructions to stack dishes in the corner cupboard.

'Careful, Georgia, your hands are shaking. You'll break the plates!' Tina frowned. 'What's the matter with you?'

'Sorry,' said Georgia, gripping them tighter.

When she finished, the boys had disappeared. She wanted to ask Mark to walk her home, but she couldn't find him in the house.

The crooked screen door at the back of the house stuttered open at her touch. Georgia paused and peered into the darkness. She heard the anxious clatter of the eucalypt trees that crowded the long, narrow yard, but the pale, swinging light in the kitchen only reached to the bottom of the high timber stairs. The moon hung low, its dim crescent bleeding an indifferent glow, leaving the yard asphalt-black.

'Where's Mark?' she asked Tina. 'It's after dark and there isn't a light in your shed.'

'What? Need your big brother to take care of you? You're such a baby. We're going to have some fun, but I guess goodie-two-shoes will want to ruin it.' Tina shoved Georgia aside. Georgia swallowed hard.

'I just ... '

'They're outside.' Tina laughed. 'We're going too, we're going to play "the game", *you know*.'

'I ... I ...' Georgia pointed vaguely in the opposite direction; inside the house. She retreated, stumbling against the kitchen table.

'Suit yourself.' Tina ran lightly down the steps into the darkness.

Georgia fled inside. It was quiet in the house, except for the *tuck, tuck* of the loud clock. In Tina's room, she opened the wardrobe and slipped in. She wriggled in the cramped confines, pushing shoes aside.

It seemed like hours had passed without a sound. Georgia's head jerked as she fought sleep.

Tina hadn't come in the room since she'd made one rushed trip to call out, 'Georgia, where the hell are you? Oh, who cares'. Georgia thought of the warm fire at home, dancing colour onto the walls through the stained-glass panel of the fire screen. Mum brushing her hair exactly one hundred strokes, Dad reading the paper and responding 'Hmm?' whenever Mum said something. They'd be in bed now.

She didn't know the time, but it was horribly, *horribly* late in this strange house where parents seemed to fade into crooked rooms through faded, thick-papered walls. Slipping the wardrobe door open a fraction, she saw that all the lights were out. Tina's bed was still empty. She crept out and slipped silently beneath the faded, red covers of the guest bed, winding the rough blankets tightly around her with bleached-cold fingers.

Georgia woke to harsh morning light, instantly alert, surprised she'd fallen asleep. She hadn't heard a sound. Not even Tina coming into the room and crawling into bed. She threw the covers back, grabbed her backpack, thrust her shoes on and ran, not even glancing to see if Tina was awake.

'Jeez Tina, you'll scrub the lino bare. What gives?' said Kyle.

The old washing machine clattered and thunked in the background. Large piles of dirty laundry littered the kitchen floor, waiting for Tina's attention.

'The little bitch is gone,' said Tina.

'What d'you mean, gone?' Kyle asked.

Tina raised herself, clutched at a cramp in her back and threw the scrubbing brush into the bucket. 'She went home. She was gone when I woke up.'

'What? Why? The weekend's hardly started.' Kyle's face paled. 'Will she ... tell?'

'There's nothing to tell. She's a prissy-know-nothing!'

'Then why'd she go home? Hey?' Kyle leaned close, his hot breath searing. 'You'd better fix this; tell one of your stories.'

'I didn't say anything. She doesn't know anything.'

Kyle grabbed her ponytail, pulling her head back. 'Get the little bitch into trouble real good.'

'Yeow! Leave me alone!' Tina met Kyle's angry, blue eyes. Their guilt sparked like flint.

Tina returned to the housework, her mind coiling

around the problem. Last night's elation had faded as fury consumed her, not only for Georgia, but for her mother as well, for Tina bore the laborious upkeep of a cramped house with crooked floors.

Wan and worn, Tina's mother finally arrived at the table for Tina to serve her breakfast. Tina spilled her tearful slander. Her pleading agony did not fail.

Her mother shuffled to the phone, and after the call went back to bed, claiming migraine.

Tina was solicitous, taking her mother's tablets to her. She clicked the door shut. Her lips curved in satisfaction.

The fluorescent light in the corridor of the police station hissed into life. Georgia shivered, wanting to crawl onto her father's lap, but both parents sat in frozen silence, their faces tight, the colour of candle wax.

'Mum.' Georgia tugged on her mother's sleeve. '*Mummy*. What's wrong?'

Her mother turned and looked down, eyes curded yellow. She wrapped stiff arms around her daughter. 'It's not your fault, Baby.'

'*What* isn't my fault? Why are we at the police station?'

'It's okay, Baby,' said her father.

Two police officers approached. Georgia wanted to scream. Why were her parents calling her baby? It was late. Her head hurt with every buzz of the stammering light. A big, square policeman introduced the female officer, a tiny, dark woman with soft, brown eyes. The officers spoke. Georgia caught the words 'bringing the boys in'. Her parents nodded. The female officer smiled at Georgia, and then her mother as she ushered them into a cold, grey room. They sat on white, plastic chairs with steel legs that had scarred the cement floor.

The officer flipped open a yellow writing pad. 'Don't be afraid, Georgia,' she said. 'I just want to ask you some questions. Tina's mother phoned your mother. Your mum talked to you about that, right? Tell me about the things Tina said to her mother about the game. Can you do that for me?'

'Mum told me what Tina said to her mother. I didn't understand what Tina meant. Anyway it was lies because she talked about touching *inside*. I said to Mum, "Yuk! That's ridiculous, you can't *get inside someone*. That only happens if a doctor operates and cuts you open". I had my appendix out last year, you see, so *I knew*. I knew it was rubbish.'

Georgia's mother was strangely still, only moving a firm hand to quiet the scraping of the steel-legged chair when Georgia wriggled.

'Now, I want you to think hard and tell me what happened last night.'

'Last night?' Georgia felt a cold, hard knotting in her chest. 'I hid in Tina's wardrobe. The others were outside somewhere.'

'And before that? What do you remember?'

'I tried to help with dinner, but I wasn't much use. The others were laughing and talking, about stuff ... I made them angry, I didn't want to play "the game".'

'What game, Georgia?'

'I don't know!' Georgia collapsed against her mother.

She dragged Georgia into her lap.

'Try and remember, darling,' soothed her mother. 'Can you try for Mummy?'

'They just said "the game". Tina's brother pushed at me ... the clock talked too loud ... I mean ...' Georgia began to tremble. She stared at the gouges that criss-crossed the cement floor, caught in their depths and ugly lines.

The air in the room grew thin.

'What did the clock say, Georgia?' The officer spoke slowly, leaning into the barely-breathed words.

'... *fuck, fuck.*

Minutes later, Tina stared at the same gouged concrete floor and wished her mum was with her, as hot tears scoured her cheeks. Her father sat tensely across the table. For the first time in Tina's life, flippant words eluded her.

The heavy drapes were drawn. Only the fire gave light to the room. Georgia sat on the floor in front of her mother. Her father had put his glasses on, and picked up the newspaper, but it remained folded in his lap. Georgia's mother brushed her hair. Georgia knew she was counting, in the fractured reflection of the fire screen she saw her mother's lips moving.

• From *Coastlines 6*, Southern Cross University anthology

Dagworth Homestead

Captain Brentwood wiped rivulets of sweat from his forehead, placed his quill carefully in the worn inkwell, and massaged the cramp in his hand. He deeply regretted the absence of his constable - George Ellerton was an able scribe, and although a little rough around the edges, he at least gave an officer of the law due respect, unlike the locals who had tried his considerable patience that morning.

Looking at the sheaf of papers on his desk, he moaned. Dozens of accounts of the alleged event and not one of them alike. Although, the circumstances of his investigation hardly warranted the category of 'event'. If in fact it had occurred at all, it would be more correct to call the debacle a tragic incident, unworthy of his rank, but needs must. After all, there had been civil unrest with the shearers.

Will I ever become accustomed to this infernal heat, he thought. After two years I find myself still at the mercy of this penal colony, its wretched humidity, idle convicts, drunkards, thieves and scoundrels—not to mention the wildlife. Damned paperwork, I've been at this nonsense since sunrise. I feel like I've interviewed half the town and I still haven't interviewed the guests from the property.

Who knew a rural farm employed more servants than a Duke's manor and catered for more guests than a royal banquet? If another hired hand tells me that Dagworth Homestead is not a farm, but a substantial sheep station of great importance I will be tempted to lose my cool entirely. And, this from mere servants who object to being called maids. Is there no end to the indignity? I shall be pleased indeed to be back in the city where I know every dangerous street and each shifty villain. Not like this mad country parade of swaggering citizens who delight in leading me a merry dance. So, it only takes one generation for good breeding and high standards to fall by the wayside. Oh, who am I fooling—half of these indigents are probably fresh off convict ships.

At least in the city he was afforded the respect of his peers, and he had long been inured to the opinions of the criminal element and it mattered little what they thought of him, unless they were armed and faster than he, which was an occasion that had not yet presented itself to Captain Lloyd Brentwood, lately of Brisbane and soon to return there. Post haste if he had his way.

But fate did not appear to be smiling on his dearest wishes. With the way things were going, he would be held up for a week, instead of the few hours the incident required.

'Who's left Menzies?' he called to the casually dressed

constable who was deep in conversation with the garrulous publican who more than likely had no connection to the event, but insisted that he had 'information of great import and don't mind 'ow long I waits ter see the gentleman city officer'. Realising that he himself was in danger of losing his manners, Captain Brentwood added, 'If you please, Constable Menzies, could you bring me the list of relevant persons, and if refreshments are available I wonder if you could procure me some lunch. Also, while I have your attention, it would be indeed beneficial if you could spare me the time to peruse the names with me and inform me of the connection of the person to the ... er ... case. I don't want to waste my time speaking with individuals with the merest connection to events or those who have heard whisperings from cousins twice-removed.'

Loosening the top button of his military coat, he rose and walked to the dusty window that overlooked the street. Drovers leant on the doorway to the Public House, tankards held loosely in that casual manner he had come to know that belied innate alertness. Several men pulled their hats forward, avoiding his scrutiny, amusement etched on their faces. Hearing soft footfalls he turned. The publican had entered the room.

'If it would please yer, sir, I'd be mighty pleased to shout y'good self a meal at my Public 'ouse across the road, and I c'd tell yer me tale—er—version of the events pertaining to the night in question.' This statement was accompanied by a broad toothless smile. 'Beg yer pardon, sir, I'm Harry Garrett, business man and owner of the local...'

'I'm sorry, Mr Garrett, but I am not accustomed to

conducting matters of military investigation in public places, no offence to your establishment, of course. However, I will confer with the constable and call for you if I require a statement,' said Captain Brentwood.

Harry shuffled his red-brown hat with earnest hands, while attempting to smooth some stray strands of hair over his bald crown.

'However, I do thank you for the cordial offer of your hospitality. It just wouldn't suit. Protocol, you know.'

'Oh, of course, sir, silly of me ter...ah, we 'ave a more relaxed attitude 'ere in the country, but I sees yer intention, indeed I do. I'd be well pleased if yer'd accept a meal brought over. I'll jest get Molly to bring you a lamb roast with veg'tables.'

'I'll pay,' said Captain Brentwood, ignoring the look that passed between the publican and the constable.

Half an hour later, Captain Brentwood regretted his request for Constable Menzies to join him. Instead of a briefing on those connected to the situation, he had been regaled with what he could only call 'gossip'. And that summation was definitely charitable. The constable had taken the opportunity to fill the captain in on local unrest, the political implications of the shearers' grievances, which would have been annoying at any time, but was made all the more discomforting because the ebullient man had sought responses to his verbose expostulations and Captain Brentwood did not like to be interrupted when partaking of a meal. To the captain's surprise the repast was superior in every way.

'So Menzies, what you're saying is that I should see

everyone on this list?' Captain Brentwood's patience was wearing thin.

Constable Menzies nodded.

'Oh, alright. But who's this Banjo Patterson fellow? What sort of a name is Banjo? I've never seen such a parade of time-wasting...'

'He's a poet, Captain.'

'A *what?*'

'A poet, sir. Aye, I'll admit he's not what one usually expects of a poet. He writes bush ballads. He's not of the style of that poncy poet Lord Byron, of course, but in these parts ... well the whole nation really, he's considered somewhat of a celebrity. Very popular fellow...'

Captain Brentwood's eyes narrowed. Was the constable deliberately baiting him? Would like day never end? Rising to his feet in what he hoped what a dismissive manner he said, 'And when may we reasonably expect this Banjo chap to grace us with his presence?'

'Well, er...' The constable squirmed. 'It's hard to say, sir. I hear he's presently engaged in assisting the town Reverand choose a right piece of horseflesh at the local saleyard.'

'Oh, never mind. Is anyone waiting...' Seeing the constable stumble for a response, Captain Brentwood strode across the room, 'Don't worry, Menzies, I'll see to them myself.'

Brentwood scanned the long corridor. There, on an array of chairs, was what could only be described as a veritable crowd of people. A lively crowd at that. His writing hand cramped with dread. Taking a deep breath he began the interviews. Life in his Mother country, where gaining information was akin to pulling teeth, had not prepared the captain for a noisy mob of people from all walks of life eagerly waiting to offer their statements.

'It was well on nigh over a year ago,' said Mrs Argeton, the cook from Dagwood Homestead, 'if one listened to local rumour, and I must make it clear that I am not one of those idle gossipy women, it would appear some poor fellow drowned himself out at the Combo Waterhole. There are others that have a different view, of course. Why Harry Garrett over at The Drover's Arm would be your best source for all the variations... Have you met our publican?'

'Yes, Madam, I have had the ... er ... pleasure just this morning. However, I am trying to separate the facts from fiction and innuendo.'

'Oh Lordy,' laughed Mrs Argeton, 'you sound like that poet fella with them big words. And don't stand on ceremony with me, young man, I'm known as Mrs around here. We've no truck with airs and graces.'

'Right. Certainly Mrs Argeton. So can you tell me anything that you saw or witnessed firsthand?'

'Oh Captain, I never laid eyes on any of that nonsense. Why isn't it my place to be in the kitchen? I'm lucky enough to see the inside of m'own house in daylight with all the work I do. Not that I'm complaining mind you, the Macpherson's are a lovely family. Why, Mrs Macpherson even gave me the day off with pay to come in here to help.'

Mrs Argeton leaned forward, her eyes clouded.

Captain Brentwood paused before speaking again. 'So, the only thing you can tell me is that this incident of the shearers' strike and the burning of the shearing shed occurred a year ago?'

'Why, Captain, never did I say such a thing. It was a year ago that Mr Paterson visited with the Macpherson family. The fire that destroyed the shed happened months before, in September, the beginning of spring.'

'And what does the visit of Mr Paterson have to do with anything?'

Mrs Argeton bristled. 'I don't know that I understand your meaning. Mr Paterson was a guest.'

'Was he present at the time of the fire?'

'I don't know all the comings and goings of guests. I'm told how many people will require meals. Sometimes I know who is there, but often I don't.'

'But you know about the visit in January of 1894?'

'Well, yes, there was great excitement. That was when Mr Paterson wrote a wonderful poem. He called it 'Waltzing Matilda'. Miss Christina remembered a piece of music she'd heard while she was in Victoria. Mr Paterson was quite taken with the music and worked his poem to set with it. So it's not just a poem really, but a true bush ballad, and if I'm not mistaken it will become quite as famous as Mr Paterson's other writing. There's...'

'Mrs Argeton, I would implore you to stick to the facts in hand. I am here to investigate the death of Samuel Hoffmeister who allegedly set fire to the woolshed at the homestead. They tell me he was known as "French" or "Frenchy".'

'Well, why didn't you say so? What would I be knowing about the shearers, for don't they have their own quarters and shearers' cook? I don't know anything about that. Can

I take my leave, now?'

Captain Brentwood sighed. 'Yes, of course, Mrs Argeton.'

'Menzies!' he shouted. The constable scurried into the room, giving the distinct impression he'd been listening at the door.

'Yes, sir.'

'Could you please take another look at *your* list, and send away those with no knowledge of the night in question.'

'Do you want me to interview them first, Captain?'

'Of course not.'

'Then how am I to ascertain whether they know anything about the death of Mr Hoffmeister?'

'Well, at least get me the doctor who signed the death certificate.'

'That's not possible, Captain. Old Doc Parsons died nigh on six months ago now. Fond of a tipple he was. Liver got him in the end.'

'The records?'

'Here's the thing. That's just as much a mystery as the dead man. There must have been a death certificate – or that's what we assumed, but no-one has ever been able to turn one up.'

The afternoon progressed in a most unsatisfactory fashion. Menzies had perused the list and only dismissed one person.

The owner of Dagworth Homestead was an affable chap

who volunteered a gratuitous amount of information about sheep farming and the superior quality of Australian wool. 'Our country lives on the sheep's back, Captain,' he said. 'But I know nothing about Samuel Hoffmeister's death. He's buried here in town, I know that much. He was one of my shearers, surly sort of fellow. Fond of a bit of biffo, especially after a night at the public house. I was busy attending to the fire. Terrible blow that was – watching the shed burn down, hearing the sheep – not able to do much more than form a line with half a dozen metal buckets. No farmer likes to see his animals suffer like that, even if it's necessary to send some to the slaughterhouse. Cruel end for them.'

'I'm afraid you are rather veering from the point, sir.'

'I'm trying to say that not everyone can take living here. The shearers can be a belligerent lot. It's a shocking thing when men burn down a woolshed that provides their livelihood. It's a harsh country, that it is, Captain. There's none of your hedgerows and thatched cottages with rose gardens blooming all year 'round and greenery for miles like you're used to – it's dusty and windblown, red dust at that. Near chokes a man. If there isn't a drought where the ground is too parched for a solitary blade of grass, there's a deluge that washes the sheep and all in it's wake. Then there's the bushfires. You don't know despair until you've seen these things, Captain. Australia, land of extremes. But I guess you know that – been here a while have you?'

'I fail to see how the geography, or the weather has anything to do with the death of Samual Hoffmeister, and I find your attitude less than helpful. I am an officer of the

Crown investigating a death. If you have nothing to enlighten me on the matter at hand I will take up no more of your time, sir.'

Captain Brentwood damped down his frustration. He hadn't wanted to come to Winton, but a soldier didn't question his superiors. Over a year had passed since the burning of the woolshed and the death of Hoffmeister. If the truth was hidden there was little prospect of it coming to light.

When questioned, Menzies informed the captain that the troopers who were rumoured to have pursued the hapless Hoffmeister had all vowed they were together on the night and were miles from Winton, checking into a report of a bank holdup by bushrangers. There was even a scrawled entry in the police records. Two of the troopers had returned to England and the other had been posted to 'somewhere in the Northern Territory'.

The head shearer had nothing to offer, he was newly appointed, and the shearers quarters were empty. The itinerant workers were working at other employment, most likely as jackaroos, logging or working on the railways. The shearers' mechanic was not available. He was only in town during the shearing season, which was over for the year.

The new doctor who had taken over Doc Parsons office was more than willing to see the captain, but he declared that there was no record that Hoffmeister had ever been a patient, much less information on the man's death.

The sons of the owner of Dagworth Homestead were relaxed, casual fellows who spoke with much bravado of their tussle with death and destruction fighting the fire in the huge woolshed.

Captain Brentwood was weary. The constable had just brought him a tankard of ale when he heard a melodic female voice. A fashionable lady strode into the room. She appeared to be in her early twenties, and smelt of soap and fresh flowers. Flicking her gloves off quickly she gave the captain a brisk handshake. 'I'm Christina Macpherson,' she said, and sat in the chair opposite the desk without waiting for an invitation. 'Am I the last person you need to interview?'

'I wouldn't say need...' The Captain sighed. 'But no, I still have to see that poet fellow.'

'Oh Barty, you'll like him.'

'Barty? I thought his name was Banjo.'

'That's just the name he writes under – he chose it because of a racehorse, you know. His name is Andrew Barton Paterson.'

The captain raised a quizzical eyebrow.

Christina continued, 'He listened to a song I played and wrote a poem for it. Did you know that? It's been published in the papers and it will be made into sheet music soon. It's marvellous.'

There was an artlessness about the woman. Her eyes lit up with the telling of the tale. In spite of himself, Captain Brentwood found himself overtaken with curiosity.

'Does he write many songs? I thought he was a poet?'

'Oh, Barty is much more than a poet. He was a practising solicitor – I think he began writing in his student days. But this bush ballad, 'Waltzing Matilda' is the first one set to music.' Her smile was beautiful. The captain found himself smiling in return.

'But you don't want me to go on about that. I must warn you that I shall be of no use whatsoever to you. I was in Melbourne at the time of the fire in the great woolshed. Barty wasn't here either, he travels prodigiously, much the same way as he writes.'

'You are refreshing Miss Christina, you're the first to admit that you don't have any information to assist the investigation.'

'Oh dear, not much happens here in the country, *usually*. I s'pose you've had every gossip in town bending your ear.'

'In the interest of discretion I won't comment.' The captain leaned back in his chair and smiled. 'So this 'ballad', it's a Waltz tune...?'

'Oh no,' laughed Christina, 'The song is about a swagman – they're out-of-work fellows travelling all over looking for work. The swaggie in the song steals a sheep, and rather than be taken in by troopers he jumps into the billabong and drowns.'

The captain laughed, 'Not a romance then.'

'Not at all. Other than the romance of the land. Barty has a wonderful way of conveying Australian life.'

'So why call it 'Waltzing Matilda? You must forgive a humble soldier – I have only been in the Australia for two years, and seldom in rural areas.'

'Oh dear, I'm sorry, I'm not explaining it very well. "Waltzing" refers to travelling on foot with all of one's possessions, which describes the life of the swaggie, and "Matilda" is the Australian word for whatever he uses to carry his belongings.'

Captain Brentwood's brow furrowed. 'Hmm, I would like to say "I see", but quite frankly I don't. Although, I should very much like to hear you sing it.'

'Well, don't expect to be any the wiser when you hear the song,' said Christina. 'Are you going to offer me a drink? I'm parched ... Oh there's Barty now.' She pointed out the window to where a tall man with enviable grace was dismounting from a magnificent stallion. Andrew Barton Paterson was lean and tanned. In no manner did he fit the image Captain Brentwood had formed. As if aware of their scrutiny, Paterson turned and gazed through hooded eyes, tipped his hat and headed into the public house. Men swarmed around him with backslapping greetings.

Christina smiled at the astonishment on the captain's face. 'You don't really expect him to come in for an interview do you? He's not one to waste anyone's time – his own included. After all, he only wrote a whimsical poem, even if some claim that it's a political allegory.' She eyed the captain with barely concealed amusement. 'Although he's tremendously popular, Barty's not one to dance to any man's tune. Comes of being a nationalist, I suppose.'

'Well, it's a good thing to have an upstanding subject of King and Country.'

'Oh, Captain Brentwood. Barty's nation is *Australia*.'

29 Sorrow Street

I dreamed of Clara. Not the fourteen year old I was leaving behind, but the three year old from our days at Bethnal Green. The ragged child with tired anxious eyes, clinging to the hem of my dress as Father yelled, 'stay put the pair a yer!' Sometimes his face was more sad than angry and then he would spare a backward glance, and say in a softer voice 'take care a y'sister, Laura', before disappearing into the dark fog of the London night. Mother had already gone, scouring the streets for food, comfort—and gin.

My dream was a moaning desperation as I thrust open door after door, running from dim room to room, seeking the warmth of Aunt Bea's cottage. At one instant finding myself in one of the many rooms of Lord Barthlow's city residence where gloves and lace shawls chased me—the next instant shuffling in chains into the crowded courtroom of the Old Bailey, and then fighting the heavy gates of Newgate as they clanged ceaselessly behind me echoing through every room of my nightmare. But always with

Clara, her fearful eyes fixed on me. At last the dream quietened. We were back in the hovel at Bethnal Green. Clara's eyes fluttered in sleep as light from the dying fire cast shadows around the room. I touched her tangled blonde curls, resisting the urge to wipe the grime from her face.

A scream tore the vision from me. I murmured apology. I had grasped the hair of the woman lying beside me on the lower decks of *The Charlotte*, the ship that would deliver the sentence of transportation for seven years to the foreign shores of New South Wales for the crime of theft of one pair of child's gloves and a lace shawl.

The ships in harbour were our new prison.

Misery rose, so dark and dense I struggled to breathe. To be denied Clara, to be exiled. Home would always be Aunt Bea and Clara. I had never understood Aunt Bea's songs of homeland, but in that dark moment I longed for land and home.

Memories of home intruded as I lay shivering, with only a coarse blanket to spare me the unyielding timber deck. Sorrow and joy besieged in equal tides.

I remembered the day Aunt Beatrice and Uncle Bertram arrived in Bethnal Green. Clara and I had been woken in the middle of the night by loud rapping on the door. My heart had pounded. Father would be angry if he found the fire alight. But it wasn't Father, or Mother. They were no more.

I remembered the happiness of the rectory where Clara and I were welcomed and loved, where we were fed till our stomachs ached. Where we discovered laughter and play. The memory of my first sights and sounds would always be dreamlike. I recalled the exquisite delight of listening to Uncle Bertie's rumbling voice, his sermons and whimsical stories, of learning to read and write with him, spellbound by the new worlds within the pages of the scores of books in his library.

At the endless pitching of the ship I longed to weep. Dear Uncle Bertie, whose death has forced our eviction and servitude in the house of Lord Barthlow, Aunt Bea to the kitchen, Clara to the laundry and for me—the seamstresses room. Shame and misery tightened my chest as I fought tears. How much heartache I had caused with one careless act—borrowing gloves and a lace shawl from the mending basket so that Clara could hold her head high at a friend's birthday party. In those dark hours I questioned which delivered the most misery—memories of poverty and want, or the fleeting memories of happiness known and lost forever. As the haze of dawn crept across the ship's deck and fog horns heralded morning activity in Portsmouth harbour, I cursed every memory as my throat cramped with the ache of unshed tears.

Just as we began to think we would never set sail, there was a bustle of activity among the sailors. New officers with shine and polish and jaws set firm with meticulous intent arrived. There was a bustle of activity among the seamen. New military officers arrived, neatly uniformed with gleaming brass, their jaws set firm.

The fleet was setting off. Several of the women prisoners

who were leaving children behind began to weep piteously and beg for death, their wailing louder than the screeching gulls, the seamen's loud orders and the snap of scores of sails that stretched skyward. One poor soul even contrived, by desperate means, to throw herself over the side and dangled there screaming and bloodied, held fast by her chains.

The voyage, with its dark misery, was little improvement on the eleven long months in Newgate Gaol. The conditions of prison life surpassed even the squalor of Bethnal Green. It was in Newgate that my early torrent of tears soon learned silence. Weeping was a dangerous pastime there. Thus my eyes became iron gates to quell the tears of my homesick grieving, but the stemming of that tide of grief made my chest ache as if pressed by heavy chains. With such a crowding of bodies, wailing brought swift scorn and often brutal reward from not only our jailers but fellow inmates. Many a night I would have welcomed the surrender of my life to the fetid darkness. I could not fathom how a physical body could push so mightily to exist with a soul slowly dying within. But exist I did.

Once at sea with daily routine established, many of the officers took to writing. It would seem that a toff by the name of Joseph Banks could have been inspiration for some of their written endeavours, for the men spoke of the acclaim he received after voyaging to this new land for which we are bound, this New South Wales.

Oh, how I envied them their leather satchels, their

writing implements, but most of all the freedom to sit with casual address and have the world at large acknowledge the merit of their time spent recording the day's events. There they sat on the deck, military officers resplendent in their red coat glory, marines of His Majesty's Naval Corps and seamen more accustomed to accompanying the products of commerce.

Jimmy Pinter, a cheeky fourteen year old chimneysweep who had previously been under the tutelage of a master thief for the purpose of entering the premises of the rich, was rebuffed with strenuous laughter when he asked an officer for 'sum 'o that nice ink and paper to prose a few lines to me dear old ma'. That made the men laugh. Part of the amused scorn he endured was because he was, in fact, an orphan. This state he bore with no bitterness, having experienced no other. Being a cheerful boy and keen to learn any craft of the sailors, he was well pleased to have entertained the soldiers and seamen, for they knew only too well his illiterate status, a circumstance that he vehemently expressed no wish to change. They never knew how my hands ached for that small pleasure, for it was commonly held that convicted criminals were the illiterate scum of society.

The men accepted this interruption to their journal postings, which task they applied a deal of dedication.

The soldiers didn't guard their discourse on many matters in front of convicts, and the subject of Captain James Cook and Joseph Banks was a popular one, exceeded only by the mysterious Arthur Phillip who would command the fleet. His name, however, was uttered with greater restraint and little was disclosed for convict hearing, merely that he was a man of meticulous organisation who made persuasive and persistent requests for the journey.

We never saw him, and little expected to, as the ships designated for cargo (and that included convicts) would not be carrying Captain Arthur Phillip. Later, we were surprised to find that he had managed the careful planning for the voyage from an inauspicious office on land.

From the relentless misery of *The Charlotte* with its constant movement like a rolling dream without end, with only brief snatches of the horizon on deck to relieve the tedium, I set myself to endure. I lay among the other women at night when the moaning and sighs had abated and was grateful for the small mercy of not suffering from the wretchedness of seasickness, a condition that sorely tested many.

At sea there was not one sight or sound that bore any resemblance to my previous life, the conditions surpassed the squalor even of Bethnel Green, the first home of my remembrance.

I had never seen the ocean, never travelled beyond the confines of London. The world, every aspect of it, was alien, and I the most alien being in it.

The new world was a shock in every imaginable way. There was no sign of a dwelling or any kind of building. Cheeky Jimmy Pinter inquired politely of an officer as to what the soldiers would chain us to. Occasionally we saw a dark-skinned, near-naked native. We were told that these people were very primitive and few in number, nothing worthy of consideration.

I was assigned to a senior officer, name of Randell, and his wife and children. I greeted the industry of the Randell's abode with no small relief. It is my guess that this superior circumstance was arranged because of my ability to read and write, a revelation that I had not encouraged, fearing taunts from the other prisoners.

While attending correspondence for Mrs Randell my joy at holding a writing implement knew no bounds. I could not rid myself of the notion of writing my own history.

I was able to secure a thick, brown-paper-bound book that was given to me by Mrs Randell for the purpose of recording recipes. And in this I am faithful, writing recipes from memory of dinners cooked by Aunt Bea, but also taking dictation from Mrs Randell. My private entries have been written in the centre of the book and concealed from that good woman. The manner of my devotion to this task of recording events is taxed by other pressing demands on my time, and to no less degree, the jerking of my memory as I record that which is foremost in my mind and can be best relied upon.

I started my journal somewhere near the beginning of the voyage—recalling events after we had been boarded on *The Charlotte*. This was necessary because without the means, or indeed the time to write, my thoughts and observations had to be stored as captured memories in a sometimes fevered brain.

I shall, of course, need to place it all in order at a time

when the hours of the day are mine alone—a circumstance too delicious to contemplate, or place any present hopes upon, for my days are full of toil. That particular state is not new to me, and this habit of daily grind has stood me in good stead, for it is all I have ever known. Those memories of a life denied, are all I have of the seventeen years of my life before I was arrested and dragged before the court in

My story, like any other story, begins with my birth and early life. That beginning is where I should commence and will try to address in my next entry for I have determined that I will undertake this journal in the best way open to me, even though my purpose is not so grand as the officers or seamen.

I have no aspirations of leaving missives for posterity, or to gather the fame and fortune that followed the already wealthy and connected Joseph Banks—for I am mere woman.

*Based on true events and on the facts known of the life of one of my convict ancestors from the First Fleet. Fictionalised.

Child carer

Kate couldn't remember when her role of caretaker for the family had begun. It stretched back into a childhood that should still exist, but didn't. It was a habit, pure and simple. Its beginning was unimportant. There was no clear moment to pin a memory; not like the first time her mother had waved her aside with a moan.

'Are you all right Mummy?'

Mother had turned over with a defeated shrug, burying deeper into a cocoon of dark silence.

'Feed the children.'

As if they were Kate's children and not hers. They were not Emily, Daniel and Sara anymore. And when father turned his key in the front door—*that* would be hers too.

'See to your father, Kate. There's a good girl.'

Kate had never questioned. She met her father with a smile, asked about his day and busied in the kitchen. That's what mother used to do.

At first Kate had stumbled around dropping things and fighting a tight little knot in her stomach. Toasted sandwiches were easy. Then she had learned to use the stovetop.

Father kissed her forehead.

'Where's your mother?'

'Not well today.' Said carefully and neutrally, as if pretending things were normal would make them so. Transform life into a manageable thing. As if ten year olds everywhere were the ladies of the house, the caretakers of the family.

'I see.'

Father didn't change the rhythm, so that helped make it normal. Though deep inside a much younger Kate screamed that it was not. But Emily, Daniel and Sara's voices were louder. Some inner sense stopped Kate from calling them 'the children' as was her mother's custom. She was even particular that she called them in order of their age, oldest to youngest, as if by this precision she could push back the chaos that hovered like a patient bird of prey.

The only evidence of Kate's ambiguity was in the manner she addressed her mother. When she thought of her, she called her Mother, but out loud she called her Mummy. Kate was unaware of this, of course. Children find different voices and Kate was no exception. Perhaps she wanted her mother to be Mummy like the mothers she saw at the corner store, or the ones on television. They were Kate's point of reference.

It was unavoidable then, in those places—the differences in their house, their family. At the supermarket the mothers supervised tots with strident, begging voices and errant feet. They didn't walk with hurried step and downcast eyes, feeling shame. Shame for her family, the differences, but mainly for herself. She was ashamed of being Kate, the mother.

But she could not share confidences leaning over trolleys, or wave cheery greetings. Presenting crumpled notes and thrusting the change back into her school uniform pocket, Kate had no thought but to get back to Emily, Daniel and Sara. To make sure they were safe. Back to the house. For that's what it was to her. She had surprised a boy on the school bus when he had tried to make conversation.

'Are you going home?' He had a kind face.

'I live in a house. It's 23...'

She'd bitten her lip, and stopped. It wasn't safe to tell strangers where, or when. Everyone was a stranger. She hadn't made the mistake again. A boy's baseball cap and a gaze fixed on a book had forestalled the most inquisitive of her travel companions. Those who went to the same school.

Emily sat quietly beside Kate, sheltered in the window seat by her older sister. While other children chatted, whispered and laughed, Kate wondered if she would get home before Daniel and Sara. Hoping the bus wouldn't be delayed. It was important to be there at the door when Mrs Blakehurst, their babysitter from up the road brought the younger two. It was important to use her grown up voice, through a narrow slit in the door.

'Thank you, Mrs Blakehurst. Here is your pay.' Passing a stained envelope with cash. Hoping to evade Mrs

Blakehurst's questions.

'How is your mother today?'

'She's in the kitchen. She asked me to give you this.'

Mrs Blakehurst's brow furrowed. She opened her mouth to speak.

'The money's all there, Mrs Blakehurst. Ah ... um ... Mother checked it twice.'

Mrs Blakehurst touched Kate's arm. 'You ... I mean ... your mother doesn't have to pay me every day. Once a week would be all right.'

Kate stepped back. 'It's better this way ... Father ... prefers it.' Kate bit her tongue and began to close the door, a stark smile on her face. Daniel's school bag was in the way. 'Shift your bag, Daniel. How many times do I have to remind you?'

Daniel fetched the bag. A little too quickly. His eager face showed panic.

'Thank you, sweetie, please try and remember. For m ... Mother.' Kate patted his unruly curls, her eyes filled with tenderness.

A strange look flashed over Mrs Blakehurst's round face.

Kate prayed her words and tone were convincing, unaware this was precisely what worried the woman in front of her. Surely the woman wouldn't suspect that it was Kate, and not her mother, or father who counted out the notes, folding them neatly and placing them in the envelope, then sealing it.

So many lies.

Kate bestowed a wide smile, then closed the door on the outside world. It would be easier now. This, at least was true.

Mother was asleep, or nearly so, in the daybed in the front room. Tiptoeing, Kate moved to the kitchen at the side of the house where three small faces watched her for cues.

'Emily, don't forget to change your uniform. Make sure Daniel and Sara stay around the back. I'll call you when dinner's ready. It won't be long.'

The earlier dinner was on the table, the easier things would be..

The kitchen was in the corner of the house. Its large square windows faced the yard on two sides, giving a view of the narrow side walkway as well as the backyard. Kate pulled the kitchen curtains back.

Emily was skipping, her forehead wrinkled with concentration as she counted. 'Twen-*ty* six, twen-*ty* sev-*en*.' Two year old Sara cradled her doll, her fine blonde hair fluttering in baby wisps as she sat on the step down from Daniel. Without appearing to notice her brother, Sara was, as always, never far from him. Daniel, who was four, paid her no attention as he whispered to Bob, his imaginary friend.

Kate loved this time of day. Tea was a simple repetitive affair, the same veggies and meat every night, making preparation seamless. Cheaper too.

Magenta cherry trees lined the north side of the house with their waxy shine and dense growth. The high fence at the back would allow slanted rays of afternoon sun for a while yet. Bright magenta fruit buds nestled in the forest green leaves. Soon the trees would be covered with the cream fluffy glory of the flowers, and the ground would be carpeted with their fallen beauty.

Kate slid open the windows, far enough to welcome the southerly breeze, but not past the torn section of the fly screen. There hadn't been enough money for insect repellent this week. Daniel and Sara developed large wheals from mosquito bites, so Kate taped the slash in the screen with masking tape.

Through the lush growth of the Magentas Kate could see old Mrs Wentworth filling the bird feeder while she cooed to the birds. The birds warbled their pleasure. Kate sighed. It must be wonderful to be a bird. To have someone whose daily routine provided, and cared.

Kate sighed. It was a shame they couldn't have a puppy for Daniel. Perhaps he wouldn't need an imaginary friend then. But Mother wouldn't cope.

'I can't take care of anything else. The children are enough. A mother can only do so much.'

With a natural rhythm Kate peeled the vegetables as the double boiler built up steam. She'd seen that on television. Some cooking show. Steaming kept the nourishment in the vegetables, or something like that. Anyway, it was important.

'*Kate!*' Mother's voice. Not low and apologetic, not fragmented or worn. Angry.

Kate swung around to face her mother, knocking the steamer saucepan to the floor. Steam escaped and scalded her arm. She clutched at her forearm with a tea towel. It was a useless gesture. She knew even as she did it, but Mother had that effect.

'Put some butter on it.' Mother was dishevelled, upset. 'Butter doesn't...'

Kate reached for the freezer. Mother sighed when she opened the door and took out a packet of frozen peas.

'I hope you're not going to waste those peas, Kaitlin Jane. They aren't cheap. You don't know the meaning of money. You're just a child.'

Kate winced. She applied the frozen packet to the reddened part of her arm.

'They'll still be good for dinner, Mummy.'

Mother snatched the saucepan from the floor. 'I'll get dinner. You don't know what you're doing.'

'But ... nothing's spoiled. It was just the top saucepan—I haven't put the vegetables in yet.'

Kate reached to take the saucepan.

Mother's eyes were fire.

'I don't know what this double cooking pot nonsense is. Where did you learn that? School? We're wasting good money on your education.'

Mother pushed her away from the sink and began scraping the remaining potatoes.

'But it's a public school, Mummy. They don't...' Kate stared at the floor, counting the chipped Harlequin tiles.

'Oh yes, Kaitlin Jane, I know how much you love school. But you're wasting your time. You'll be lucky to be a wife, and a housekeeper. That's our destiny. It's all women can hope for. You'll understand when you grow up.'

Emily's giggle penetrated the afternoon.

'What have you let the children do?' Mother shrieked.

Kate straightened, protective.

'Emily, Daniel and Sara are playing in the back yard. Emily changed her uniform and...'

'Quite the little boss, aren't we.' Mother cut the potatoes roughly.

Kate resisted the urge to point out an area that was still covered in dark skin.

Mother looked at her with careful eyes.

'Daniel's quiet. I suppose he's playing with that invisible friend of his. There's something wrong with that boy. Takes after his father. A dreamer.'

Kate's muscles clenched. 'He's just...'

Mother spun around. 'What? What is he?' Her eyes flashed. The knife was poised over the pan. She threw the top saucepan in the sink. 'You just made more work. Go and play with the children. But give me those peas.'

Kate handed the bag and blanched at the pain in her arm. She went outside, but she did not play.

She tugged her dress under her to protect her legs from the splintered steps. She wondered if Mrs Wentworth next door had balm for burns. It was no use thinking about that. Mother would notice. She didn't like interfering people.

'Is dinner ready? Bob's hungry.' Daniel tugged at Kate's apron.

Kate patted Daniel's head. He was too little to understand. A taut pang of protectiveness caught at Kate's heart.

'Mummy's getting dinner tonight.'

The truth. There were enough lies inside their walls. Kate imagined them whirling around like lost pieces of wind and cloud, like a bird seeking to be free, but confused by the transparency of glass.

'Oh, dinner's never as good when she makes it. Bob prob'ly won't eat much.'

Kate smiled at her younger brother, willing it to dispel the frown on his forehead, but Daniel was not so easily persuaded.

'Why can't you be our mother?'

Kate had no answer.

A crash from the kitchen drowned her thoughts.

Followed by a scream.

Emily and Sara ran to Kate. Sara clutched the hem of Kate's dress. Kate reached down to stop her sister's grasp from damaging the thin fabric, then stopped. She offered Sara her hand instead, but Sara clung tighter and sucked her thumb.

'Mummy's mad. Is she mad at us?'

'No, Emily. She's just tired.'

Daniel shook his head. 'She's mad bout evryfing.'

Kate didn't argue. Three pairs of eyes were fixed on her. She must stay calm. They needed her. Settling the two girls onto the lower seats of the stairs, she waited. Waited to see if the noise they'd heard was the beginning, or the end. It was never the middle of trouble.

Sara clung tighter to Kate's dress.

It was silent in the kitchen. Mother must have gone back to bed. Or the loungeroom. If she had stayed in the kitchen the noise wouldn't have stopped. It was a bad sign.

'I'd better check dinner.'

Sara's anxious hands pawed at her dress, but this time she worked them free.

'You don't want dinner to burn, do you?'

Three solemn faces looked back. Emily shook her head.

'You go, Kate. We'll be okay.' Emily's back stiffened.

Kate sighed. Her younger sister was learning to protect herself.

Emily put a hand on Sara's shoulder. 'Don't suck your thumb, Sara. You're not a baby.'

Sara slowly removed her thumb. 'You're not our mother. Kate is.'

Emily looked sharply at her young sister. 'Kate is not our mother. Mummy is.'

The smell of burning came from the open window of the kitchen. Kate jumped up.

'Don't fight children. It will be all right. Dad will be home soon.'

Daniel screwed up his face. 'Daddy can't cook, Kate. Even Bob knows that.'

The kitchen was empty. Kate had no time to look for her mother. The potatoes had begun to burn on the bottom of the pan. It would take her some time to scrape the dark charcoal. She would have to rescue the potatoes somehow. Tossing them quickly out of the pan into the colander, she rinsed them over and over. She placed a small piece of the crumbly flesh into her mouth. The potatoes tasted burned.

Hot tears stung her cheeks. No amount of salt or butter would disguise the taste.

One of the gas burners glowed, but there was nothing on it. The frozen vegetables sat in another saucepan, still cold.

Dinner was ruined.

The hall clock struck 6 o'clock. Kate wiped her tears with the edge of the tea towel. Usually by now, the children would have finished dinner and the tidying up would be done, leaving her with the simple task of warming her father's meal when he came home.

A key turned in the lock. Dad was home. Kate heard a rustling sound as her mother went to the door.

'Have you been drinking, Ellen?'

Dad's voice was low, weary.

'No, Bruce. Of course not. I just rinsed my mouth...' pleading.

'Don't lie to me, Ellen. Where are the children?'

Mother began to cry, soft simpering sounds.

'I've had a terrible day. The children have been so loud. So demanding. You don't know what it's like.'

Kate's stomach formed a familiar tense knot. With trembling fingers she tried to finish the dinner preparations without making a sound. She heard the thud of Dad's boots as they hit the floor. In her mind's eye, she could see her mother clinging to the front of her father's shirt.

'Bruce, please. I'm so bone tired.'

Kate cringed at the sound of her mother's desperate pleading.

'Face it, Ellen. You're depressed again. Are you taking

your medication? You can't keep doing this. It's not fair on me, on the children. It's not a trade-off, Ellen. You have bipolar. You can't spend your life waiting for the highs.'

The soft thunk of her father's footsteps was joined by the pat-pat of her mother's bare feet. Closer.

'Why is Kate cooking dinner again Ellen? She's only ten for God's sake! What the hell have you been doing? Nothing! All day, and nothing!'

Father was yelling now.

Mother's hand was raised in front of her as if to push back the words, push back truth itself. 'You make me want to scream. Do you know you make me want to do that Bruce? That you push me so far? So close to the edge?'

Mother tore at her hair.

The back screen door squeaked. Emily, Daniel and Sara stood huddled in the doorway.

Kate froze. She must stop this—this jarring of words. This sting. She must. Any words would do.

'The wall is blue.'

*From *the wall is blue*

The opus of rage

I

He waits in tense silence, hearing the stumbling footfall on the doorstep then muffled cursing as a key jars in the lock. His father is home.

He is fourteen years old, his lanky body taut as he slides from his bed to stand at the bedroom door, his head bent, leaning into the darkness. He stretches muscles that are tight from helping his mother with her evening cleaning job. It keeps food on the table.

The sound of grinding gears woke him minutes earlier. He's a light sleeper, a restless one, with the honed instincts of a soldier. Attune to the night, he listens. He fights an electric prickle of anxiety, waiting for the signs that are precursor to violence.

Violence threads through his days, even while his athletic body finds release in sport, basketball, soccer, cross country. Violence taints his nights, even the quiet ones—those somnolent stretches of peace. Because there is always a shadow. A shadow that thunders, retreats and returns.

He winces at the sound of clattering in the kitchen. He moans, tonight won't be one of those nights his father passes out on the couch.

Stay in your room, Mum—his silent prayer. He doesn't understand why she pleads, placates or why she sometimes fights back.

There is no way to comprehend why the walls of this house shape the construct of the most dangerous place he's ever known.

The police come often. His father hurls abuse at them with democratic ease.

A scraping, shuffling noise tells him one of the younger ones has been woken and is going to the toilet. His hands clench. He hears his mother's soft voice to the child, and prays his father won't hear. In vain.

It begins—the dense drama that is family life.

'Why can't you make those children obey you?'—the opening prelude to the opus of rage.

He steps into the hallway. Menace radiates from the man in front of him, he is both stranger and father. Fast, angry and drunk, his father strikes. The younger children are all awake now, screaming, whimpering; clawing at their mother's nightie.

He towers over his stocky father. Once his mere presence was enough to stop the onslaught, but not anymore. Once he merely protected, now he is aggressor.

'You're as bad as me,' his father roars.

In the morning they will work side by side, hammering, planning, building. Each in their own silence.

He will respect and honour his father. In the morning. But tonight he's measuring blow for blow.

He vows, *I'll never be like you.*

II

He paces the upstairs kitchen. He's stressed. It's been a tough week. No one seems to understand the pressure of trying to teach dozens of kids, no one in this house anyway. Not the people under his own roof. Not the woman he married after his divorce, the one who soothes and coddles her own son, as well as the baby she has borne to him. The son he dreamed of, a son to carry his name.

His wife is breastfeeding the baby now, cooing and caressing the infant's downy head. He doesn't know why but this affection grates.

'I wish you wouldn't demand feed,' he says, his voice rising. 'I don't agree with it. *On demand*, who does that? Don't you see? Kids who are demand fed are spoiled.'

He fumes. He should be the head of the house. And as for that boy, *her* fourteen year old son, the kid shows *no* respect. To anyone.

The boy's silences infuriate, prickle and crawl under his skin, eating at him, taunting him. He'd rather open rebellion, heated exchanges than this, this voiceless insolence. This arrogant obedience.

He approaches her, his anger fermenting. 'I sent that kid down to tidy the garage. What's taking him so long?'

'Maybe he doesn't know where to put your tools, your things,' she says. 'It's chaos down there.'

He stabs at her with a finger. 'I'm too busy to run a house as well as a school.' His voice is gritty, resentful. He stands at the top of the stairs and calls the boy. 'Makes my blood boil,' he mutters, clenching his teeth.

He is greeted with silence, then a shuffling sound, feet scraping. The sounds of reluctance, defiance. The stairwell amplifies the sound.

He waits. His blood is heating.

She's oblivious, sitting in the lounge that backs on to the stair railing. Still petting the baby. She'll ruin the kids, both of them. Turn them into sappy spoilt brats. He watches as the boy begins his slow ascent. He launches into a blistering tirade. The boy says nothing, not even when he is standing on the step below him.

He lands a full body blow that spills the boy down the stairs. He follows, roaring and punching. Then kicking as the boys lies still. He rains blows, vision blurred, control gone. 'Why don't you fight like a man?' he rages.

The boy whispers, *I'll never be like you.*

He hears his wife scream, an endless piercing that fractures the air. He runs back up the stairs to her. 'I only stopped hitting *that boy* because I heard you scream and thought you'd dropped MY son!'

She freezes.

He rants. He speaks of righteous indignation, of respect, of obedience. Of his own tortured childhood, his tainted past, the wounds that will never heal, the responsibility thrust on him, the weight of it. How it claws at the pit of his gut, wakes him at night at the slightest noise. Then he leaves, taking the phone and the car.

Placing the baby down with care, she runs down the stairs, heart pounding, calling her son's name. Unaware that she'd screamed, she wonders if her son is alive. She finds him, pale, cold and bleeding. Bruised and crouching. She weeps.

She weeps for wounds she can never heal, for a heart that cannot be unbroken. For a son who will now wear the scars of battle. From a man she brought into his life. She weeps for a son who will cross the bridge to manhood with a tainted, seared psyche.

She attends to him. She finds a public phone. They don't take teenage boys at the refuge. It's a new town, she knows no one. Isolation and fear claw at her stomach. She moves in a fog. Will there ever be a safe place again?

When he returns he is still fomenting. He strides the house with primal rage. He is livid, they have no idea how far they've pushed him, what they have made him become. He demands respect.

She pleads softly to take the boys and stay with her mother, 'just for a few days, to let everyone heal, get past things'.

He spins to face her. 'Walk out that door and I'll take my son, and you'll never see him again.' The air is taut with menace. He turns to glare at the boy who is standing in the corner, then slides his eyes to her. 'You won't find me, but I'll find you. Then no one else will find you.'

The boy learns to shut down, evade—a habit he'll take into manhood.

He vows, *I'll never be like you.*

Taxidermied

Tightly holding her mother's hand, six year old Tess jerked a half-skip to keep up to the brisk steps of her maternal parent. This caused a rolling rhythm that pulled Joan Durbeyfield towards the child.

Joan grimaced, but said nothing. After all, skipping wasn't the child's most annoying habit, which inevitable involved her daughter's blighted attempts at kindness, or misjudged words that escaped like an unruly torrent at the precise moment that one would wish her silent.

Tess quietly hummed a wandering composition of her own invention.

Joan had high expectations for that day. She'd never been invited to the home of her boss and his elegant wife. She was hoping for more hours and a rise in her social status from being able to describe the grand interior of the formidable mansion to all her friends and acquaintances. It was a vision she had long imagined.

No one had seen inside the opulent abode of the well-travelled, highly-respected, vaguely mysterious Eric Bentley who was rumoured to have acquired a king's ransom of precious antiquities on his travels to every corner of the globe.

Tess received the jab of an elbow when she wrinkled her nose at the musty smell as they entered.

After a dainty, but less than hearty meal, Mr Bentley offered to show Tess some of his 'wondrous' collections—'a rare treat for the child', leaving the two women to chat, his wife to list their many accomplishments and Mrs Durbeyfield to clatter her teacup nervously.

Dark-curtained, the collection room was filled with glass cabinets. There were exotic shells. Tess wondered if the sea creatures missed their homes.

Mr Bentley explained that the natives once used cowrie shells as "legal tender" 'that's money to you, honey!' He laughed.

Tess frowned.

'Course I didn't pay for 'em,' he added, bemused by the strange child.

A cabinet in the centre of the room had glass on all sides and was filled with brightly feathered birds.

Mr Bentley stretched his braces, leaned back, waiting for the child's adulation.

Tess writhed. 'Um, are they – were they?'

The man waved his arms theatrically.

'They are taxidermies my little one, once alive, now gloriously preserved.'

Tess' head filled with dizzy fog in the stuffy room.

Mr Bentley pointed to a long, low carved cabinet with slender drawers.

Tess glided her fingers along its polished surface.

Sensing success at last, the man opened the top drawer with a flourish, anticipating the child's inevitable gasp of pleasure. Row upon row of brilliantly hued butterflies were skewered to a board with nail-like pins.

Tess ran from the house and threw up on Mrs Bentley's prized gladiolas.

Drawing a ragged breath Tess noticed the flowers. Her mother had long competed with Mrs Bentley and her prized gladiolas, each vying for the showiest floral arrangement for display beside the parson's pulpit.

Unknown to Mrs Joan Durbeyfield, Mrs Bentley employed the services of a gardener. Unknown to Mrs Bentley, Mrs Durbeyfield traded turnips and beans with a neighbour expert in floral beautification.

Tess cared for none of this. A crime against butterflies had been heinously committed, lured to their deaths by nectar, dainty wings trapped by nails. She whispered to a cheerful garden gnome, 'If people didn't collect 'em, they wouldn't have to die'. Chewing on her lip she peered into the garden shed. Aha!

Tess' mother was in fine spirits on the walk home, even humming along with her daughter, who seemed a little pale.

A week later a note arrived from Messrs. Bentley Inc. Mrs Joan Durbeyfield's services were no longer required.

Apparently, the gladiolas had withered.

An apology from Tess was required. Head down, Tess

walked along the dusty road to the mansion. A tall boy stood in her way, grinning, refusing to let her pass. Tess ignored him.

The boy kissed her soundly and ran.

'Eew!!' Tess wiped her face.

Outside the mahogany door of the Bentley mansion, disturbed and trembling from the invasive kiss, Tess tapped the brass knocker softly. The bravado before setting off had evaporated. Once facing Mr Bentley, she wept.

The man gingerly patted the child's head as she cried and hiccupped through a much rehearsed, but sadly incoherent apology.

'Hush, child, hush.'

'But I shouldn't ... and I was ... and ... sad... I only wanted ... to fix the the bu bu bu ...'

'...Bugs,' interjected Mr Bentley, finding himself so discomforted by the child's emotional display that his only wish was for its termination. He put up a hand to signal an end to her sorry state. 'Bugs, of course, you sprayed the bugs, not knowing the flowers would die.'

This new interpretation of events was partly true, so Tess nodded, grateful for the reprieve.

Anyway, my pet,' he said, ushering Tess to the door, 'a beautiful apology.'

Tess' father took her onto his knee, gave her an enquiring look with a tilt of his balding head. And, because everything secret must be whispered and not spoken, Tess murmured, 'That man murders small creatures, and, and—butterflies. **Butterflies!!**

'Oh, not butterflies,' said her father.

'There was a big red Mortein pumper thing, like the one you use, Daddy, so I took away the nectar ... because you know, Daddy, that butterflies only drink, they don't eat.' Tess tapped his head, 'and, and, there's more! **That man** wants all the cowrie shells in the world.'

Father rolled his eyes as Tess mimicked Eric Bentley's deep, rolling voice—'that's money to you, honey!'

John Durbeyfield hid a smile behind his hand and decided to give his lecture on the Care of Other People's Personal Property some other day. Moral crusades clearly took priority for his soft hearted girl.

*From *Butterfly Pinning*.

A grievous thing

'It is so tiresome to escape one's governess, don't you find, Cousin Eloisa?' said Jane, as both girls sat swinging their legs from the low thick branch of a spreading oak. 'Thank goodness it is summer—in winter the trees are next to useless for hiding places.'

'I guess it could be a nuisance escaping one's governess, Cousin Jane, but as I have so recently acquired one—courtesy of your generous family, I have not yet found it more than an entertaining pastime. And "escaping", as you call it, has helped us discover the most magical places, like this marvellous old oak tree,' said Eloisa. 'You know, cousin, it seems quite at odds with polite convention to call one's governess by her surname, especially as Gantry is such a horrible name. I wonder, do all the gentry follow that custom? It is all very confusing for a newcomer, but I must say that on first impression, a governess seems more concerned for the well-being of her charges than one's own mother would. Of course, as an orphan, I know nothing of that.'

'Oh, I am so sorry, Cousin Eloisa. I did not intend to bring up your sadness or refresh your grief, how thoughtless of me. Please forgive me.'

'Now, **that** is tiresome, dear Cousin Jane. Pity is a grievous burden. You cannot imagine how dreadful it is for everyone to constantly cast you in the light of an eternal victim of tragic circumstances. Is that how I am to be introduced for the rest of my life? Is that all people will ever whisper about? Will I ever be simply me, Eloisa Lancaster? I wonder if I shall ever shake it off. Perhaps I could move to France...'

Jane frowned. 'You know, Cousin Eloisa, you are really rather odd.'

'Well, that is a far better description to live with. You know, Cousin Jane, I think you are on to something. If I develop an interesting persona, people will have something else to focus on. I would rather be known for any number of eccentricities than as a poor soul blighted by life, and fit for nothing but pity in society.'

Jane was perplexed. Her cousin had only been living with them for several months and had given no sign of this new alarming side of her character. Jane had enjoyed the seemingly endless trips to seamstresses and fashion houses and had been overjoyed at each new acquisition. The girls had come home laden with silk dresses, velvet purses and fetching millinery confections. To be fair cousin Eloise had shown a humble and entirely appropriate gratitude. But she had chosen to wear her everyday muslin dresses whenever she could. And it was obvious that Eloise had a greater interest in the subjects of her male cousins than in pianoforte, watercolours and embroidery, for which she displayed a worrying indifference and lack of aptitude.

After an initial feeling of finally having the sister-in-spirit she had always longed for, and deciding that she and Eloisa were as near to kindred spirits as two people could be, she was shocked to realise that she did not understand her cousin at all. Never short of a word, she now found herself speechless and was rather pleased when their portly governess appeared over the hill, with her long aprons and skirts held high, sweating profusely. Heaving herself in front of the two girls, Gantry pressed one hand on her ample bosom and panted. Her face was red with exertion as she fanned her face with a muslin handkerchief.

Jane leapt out of the tree, instantly contrite.

'You frightful girls! Why do you play these games? Gallivanting all over the estate. You shall return to the house this instant and sit quietly reading, while I retire to my room to recover.'

Jane opened her mouth to apologise, but Eloisa cut in, 'If it is all the same to you, dear Gantry, I will repose awhile in the midst of the splendour of this magnificent monument to nature. After all, only minutes before we left to "occupy ourselves until nuncheon" as you instructed, you told us that we would ruin our eyes if we read another paragraph. I am new to having a governess and do not wish to give you any cause for concern. I am sure you will be pleased that now we have gallivanted all over the estate you can forego our afternoon ambulation. I shall wish you sweet rest, dear Gantry. I will certainly be back in the, er, nursery, when you awaken and arise.'

With that, Eloisa focused on an interesting spot on the horizon and began to hum.

Jane was incredulous and Gantry stood open-mouthed with shock.

'Well, I never!' huffed Gantry. 'I am sure I do not know what to say to your High and Mightiness Miss Eloisa. We shall see about this.' Firmly grasping Jane's hand, she turned to leave.

Jane threw Eloisa a disconcerted look.

Eloisa winked.

*From *Scarlett doesn't live here anymore.*

That madness

I watch them. Four men of differing ages and race. Bolstered against the wind's bluff toss, grim-eyed, unflinching. They accept four wreaths, golden circles of floral purity. One blinks a tear, refusing its course. They step forward as one to lay the flowers on marbled perfection.

Statesman and serviceman alike repeat the act of worship, row upon row. Not marching like the men they honour, but in step, in sync.

The incongruous mix of voice that formed the past few days has died—that frail bridge connecting us. For now the sharing of hot mugs, the laughing chatter, the bright-eyed wonder is last night's memory, retreating when the first rays of dawn stilled the earth. Curded clouds that ruled the night have been shredded like shards of fairy floss and melted across the sky. The sea trembles, between calm and rippling. Lost somewhere between today and a century ago—April 25, 1915 at Anzac Cove. It's a place of rare beauty. It should have been the amphitheatre to heaven.

The Aegean lapped gently on that distant day until a gunshot rang out across the water, into the disembarking troops. Chaos followed. The sound of bullets became a staccato crescendo, forming a shocking concerto of death. Men scrambled ashore searching for shelter on the fragile boundary of hell.

Someone, some VIP reads a letter; a soldier's memories of war. My eyes sting, I have no letters from my father. A regret.

I feel the page in my pocket, test its dimensions, its folded symmetry. How innocuous it seems in the depths of my jeans. But how portentous. I've won a lottery – I've been called up for National Service like my father before me. I struggle to return to the solemnity of the image in front of me. A life's dream to come to Gallipoli fulfilled, a debt of honour willingly sought and paid. For my dad, a Vietnam vet. One of the men standing before the dais represents those who fought in Vietnam. 'That madness', as Dad said. He'd won the lottery too. I wonder what he'd say. If he was here.

The mood changes after the service. I shun the crowds talking photographs and sealing friendships made in this place with promises and exchanges. The letter weighs too heavily on my mind for simple human interaction. I must decide. But not here. Not on this ground.

Mum meets me at the airport. She sobs in my arms. She weeps not for my absence and safe return, or not that only, she weeps for my conscription. My call to arms.

I offer to drive us home, but she shakes her head. I ask

her if she needs a minute.

'I need a lifetime,' she responds.

She straightens up, links her arm through mine. There is steely resolve in her eyes now. I've seen that look before, so many times: when we kids were ill, when a neighbour needed shelter from an abusive husband, but mainly when Dad was laid low with depression. There wasn't a term for it then. Post Traumatic Stress Disorder. Mum said it was a relief when they gave it a name.

But it was a term she never used. 'Your Dad's in a dark place,' she would say. 'Memories of war.'

We try to keep up small talk on the drive home, but banter is hard when most of what hangs in the air stays beneath the surface. I know the words trapped inside Mum's head, how afraid she is they will all tumble out the wrong way. 'I haven't decided yet, Mum,' I say, answering the question she dares not voice.

'Your father would still be here ... if ...' her voice trails off.

'How's Pa?' I ask.

'Oh, your grandfather's fine,' she says, 'pretty riled up at the moment though. The red-headed kid has been bothering him again. Pa thinks the kid has been stealing petrol from his scooter.'

I laugh. Pa has been waging war with the neighbours for decades. First it was the Boardmans, whose standard of house and yard maintenance didn't include using a lawn mower. Pa would sit in his canvas deckchair with his .303 and pick off rats that came through the fence. 'Bloomin' neighbours! Those grubs don't even put their rubbish bins out for pickup,' Pa would say, 'God only knows what the inside of that dump is like'. Pa thought his worries were over when the Boardman house sold, 'good riddance to bad rubbish' he said. But then a red-headed kid from a few streets away began to 'terrorise the neighbourhood'.

'Pa hasn't threatened to shoot him, has he?' I worry about how the law would deal with a ninety-six year old man who shot a feral teenager. By accident of course.

'Of course he has.' Mum smiles. 'He'd love to see you.' She sighs, torn between wanting and not wanting me to talk about war with my grandfather. Pa served in the Second World War.

Night sounds are pretty scant at Pa's place in the bush. I hear the rustle of monstera delicisio near the front door as a southerly wind teases. A barn owl celebrates the darkness. The house is silent. A dim glow leaks through the cracks in the old timber shed that serves as garage and tool shed. I struggle to open the side door.

'What the bloody hell!' Pa's voice sears the night. 'Who's that?'

'It's me, Damien. Open up Pa.'

I hear scuffling noises, then the door gives way. Pa sits in his deckchair with his rifle across his knee. His glasses are skewed and he's barefoot. I wonder at this. He's never without boots, usually Army issue. I look down at his foot and a piece of string is tied to his big toe. The end is cut and another piece of string hangs loosely from the old brass doorknob.

'I'm waitin' for that bloody red-headed kid,' he says, 'as

soon as he tries to open the door I'll let him have it. Whammo! Flamin' kid is stealin' m'petrol. Can't keep refillin' me scooter—costs a small fortune. What're y'laughin' at?'

'You, Pa. You never carried a gun through an entire war and now you're lying in wait with a rifle for some redheaded kid.'

'Only gonna scare him.' He laughs and slaps his thigh.

We talk of war while he trims a lantern. It's another world in here with Pa, another time. I tell him of my fears, my repulsion for taking human life, my worries for Mum, my trip to Gallipoli. I ask why he chose to be a non-combatant. He served as a medic. I tell him I don't know what to do.

'Only you can decide, son,' he says, rubbing his rheumy knuckles. 'I stood shoulder to shoulder with the men carryin' guns, then I carried 'em out, bullets whizzin' past, thinkin' the next one had my name on it. I respected those men, never judged their decision, and they never judged mine. I was lucky that way, I guess. Respect is an important thing in war. But for me, well...' he paused, 'there are things you see that you can't unsee in a war. I knew that, knew it before I went, knew I'd never be able to erase those images. But I didn't want to come home wantin' to undo things I'd done. The act of killin' a man. That's not mine to decide. So I carried 'em; carried 'em home.'

- Legacy University Prize, 2017.

Estrangement

George Carter had been summoned to sort out the family home at Black Mountain. Their father, Bill Carter had been dead for a year. George had delayed his role as executor of his father's will to give his three sisters time to recover, but the oldest two, Lydia and Claire were anxious for things to be settled. They had arranged to meet George at the family homestead where Susan, the youngest, was living with her disabled husband Eric and two sons.

The older Carter sisters, Lydia and Claire, sit—poised, at the blunt table in the old family home. Sly glances spoke of synchronised undertones—sisters dominating the room as they once did as teens. Both married up, and remained there, leaving Black Mountain and the life they shared as children far behind.

Susan the youngest was nervous and pale. She faltered as she placed cups of tea in front of her sisters.

Lydia shot Susan a sharp glance then turned to George.

'Will this take long, George?' She stirred the tea vigorously, spilling some into the saucer.

'Is something wrong with the tea?' Susan asked.

'The tea's fine.' Lydia tipped the tea from the saucer into the cup with an oddly defiant gesture that confused Susan.

Susan was too young to remember the running hostilities between Lydia and their mother, too young to remember Claire's aloofness and embarrassment at having a simple country mother with work roughened hands.

'Well, George. You have the floor. Anytime you're ready.' Lydia swirled her tea. Feigned airs of the past had become practised elegances.

Claire registered her disdain by merely sipping, then reached out and touched Susan's hand with light fingers. Susan leaked a smile, hungry for the affection the gesture promised, but cold eyes failed to deliver.

George leaned back in his carved dining chair, sipping his tea slowly, observing his sisters, surprised that so little had changed. He was there to do his duty—what that duty involved according to Lydia and Claire was as clear as if it was etched on the old square dining table.

The older girls were so confident of the outcome they'd left their upwardly-mobile spouses behind, secure in the belief George would serve their interests, as he once did.

'We're all here then,' Lydia said, pushing.

Claire leaned forward, spilling her tea.

Susan wiped it quickly with a tea towel.

Lydia's lips curled in distaste, 'Susan, *not with that.*'

George was taking his time and it grated on their nerves,

'The house won't be sold.' The words dropped like stones. 'Susan and Eric and the boys will continue on here.

The house is theirs. After all, they cared for both parents.'

Claire gasped, then gripped her fancy purse with white knuckled fingers.

'What the hell!' Lydia, white-angered, blanched with shock.

Susan sobbed into a balled serviette—crushed shapeless by pale hands.

'Ken will have something to say about this,' Lydia said.

'We'll get a solicitor.' Claire found her voice.

Susan turned white with shock. Her hands trembled.

It was only moments before both women turned on her as Claire pointed an accusing finger. 'You. You put him up to this, didn't you Susan. With your needy simpering ways, always running to big brother George.'

'That's enough, Claire.' Eric, Susan's husband's voice rasped as he limped across to her, dragging the leg the tractor crushed.

The slip-slide burr of the sound of Eric walking to Susan's side was the only noise in the room for a long minute.

'You haven't heard the end of this George.' Claire moved towards the door with angry precision, taking her gloves from her purse slowly and jerking them on.

'It will do you no good.' George leaned back in the chair. 'It's done. Let that be an end to it. But if not, then go ahead, do your worst. With your husbands.'

Lydia scrambled around in her purse.

She removed a slender gold cylinder from her purse and twisted it, revealing blood red lipstick.

One hand held a gold mirror as she applied the lipstick

with care, stretching thin lips, ooh, aah, with slow precise movements.

War had been declared.

*From *The lost stories of Lucy Meredith Carter*

The knowing

Miranda couldn't have told anyone when the knowing began. It was an essence as familiar as her own face in the mirror, or the colour of her eyes. She had always known too much, felt too much.

When she had watched the woman across the road snap stark white sheets off the line, she had known. In the sultry afternoon with heat rippling from the tar on the road, while the blush of the low globe of the sun bathed the woman with light, she had known. The woman paused to press the sheets to her face, savouring the scent of sunshine. A car had arrived. Two solemn policemen approached the woman. They took their caps off and placed them under their arms. They spoke in low murmurs. The woman fell to her knees, spilling the clean washing onto the ground as her heart fractured. Then the woman had known what Miranda knew, she was a widow.

Miranda heard the details later in huddled adult conversations, overheard in frozen corners of the house, where words were sharp jabs of disbelief.

'I knew,' she said to her mother, as she helped peel the potatoes for dinner, perched on the stool that gave her access to the worn timber kitchen bench.

'Knew what, sweetie?' Her mother snapped crisp ends from garden-fresh runner beans.

Miranda handed her mother a potato to inspect for missed skin. 'I knew Mr Campion had died. I knew it when Mrs Campion was taking the sheets off the line.'

Her mother stilled. She turned to her young daughter, hands poised. There was a crease between her eyebrows, a worried look. 'Miranda, whatever do you mean?'

'I knew ... before ...'

Mother dropped the beans and gripped Miranda's shoulders firmly. 'Don't say that. Do you hear me? No one knows these things. Promise me you won't talk like that again.' The crease in her forehead deepened.

Miranda nodded.

Mother's face softened. The pressure cooker hissed. A curl of steam spiralled, releasing the aroma of perfectly cooked corn on the cob. 'You must be careful with pressure cookers, Miranda,' she said. Mother said 'be careful' a lot.

Mother didn't bring the subject up again, but Miranda noticed she pressed her lips together tightly when one of her women friends visited in the calling room, especially if there was bad news. Miranda knew this was because of the knowing, but Mother didn't understand. Miranda didn't only know about bad things.

She had meant it when she promised not to talk about the knowing. It was important to Mother, it had upset her, so it would probably upset other people. Miranda didn't want that. Despite her best efforts, she tripped up. Mrs Ingleburn, the next-door neighbour but one, was young and newly married. She came to visit and was too excited to sit in the soft comfort of the faded tapestry lounge chairs. Her pretty face was flushed.

'I'm expecting,' she said, patting her cheeks to hide the pink blush of them.

Mother gave Miranda her "don't you have somewhere else to be" look, and hugged her friend. Miranda hopped from foot to foot, then headed towards the door to the dining room. She hesitated. She liked Mrs Ingleburn. It wouldn't be polite to leave without saying something.

'When are the baby boys due?' she asked.

Both women turned and stared. Miranda looked down and rubbed her shoe on the tasselled rug.

'Stop that, Miranda. You'll scuff your shoes.'

'Sorry Mum.'

'She's a funny little thing,' said Mrs Ingleburn as Miranda left the room.

Nothing was said when twin boys arrived at the Ingleburn house seven months later, but Miranda caught mother watching her with wary eyes.

On her first day at school, lined up with all the other girls with their checked uniforms all pleated precisely the same way, wearing the same brand new shoes, Miranda felt more different than she ever had before. All the sameness made it clearer.

The knowing made Miranda uneasy. She didn't like watching her favourite teacher absently caress the petals of the rose her fiancé had given her, knowing he would break her heart that very evening by calling off the wedding. Miss Chambers sat at the front of the class smiling brightly at them all. Miranda's chest squeezed tight. Then, the next day, when she saw Miss Chambers' stiff tension and red-rimmed eyes, she felt guilty as if knowing made her complicit somehow. Miranda left a handful of wild violets, tied with a ribbon on her teacher's desk, but it didn't make her feel any better. She wondered how it was that feeling deeply connected to the inner parts of other people's lives could make her feel so ... separate.

Winter's solemn chill surrendered to the zephyrs of spring, then summer. One morning, Miranda was teased awake with the lyric of birdsong, earlier than usual. She'd forgotten to close the curtains and lay entranced as dust floated in the morning sun. She felt lighter, happier. It had been a long time since she'd been worried by knowing things.

At school, for the first time, the numbers paraded across the page in effortless rhythm, instead of ending up as two, or perhaps three answers and making Miranda chew her nails in frustration. This was a very good thing because Mother had given the teacher a bottle of foul-tasting nail-paint to help break the 'dreadful' habit. She was picked early for teams in sport instead of standing alone acutely aware of herself.

The storm hit as Miranda stepped onto the grass in their front yard. The sky was stretched taut as the wind made nervous chatter in the leaves. Miranda looked up, awed by the magnificence of nature. Gunmetal clouds had gathered, dropping large soft rain, as the sun continued to shine in slanted corridors of light. Miranda spread her arms and spun, revelling in the cool pure tears of heaven. She heard a giggle behind her. A tiny dark haired girl was watching and clapping her hands. Miranda smiled. The girl joined the dance. Their laughter outlasted the thunder as the brief storm passed, leaving a cerulean sky.

'Il mio nome ... Rosa,' said the girl, her voice rumbling over the 'r' in her name. She shook raindrops from long spirals of hair.

'I'm Miranda.' Miranda looked across the road. There was a large removal van and men with laughing faces carrying a long table into a large brown-brick house. 'Wow, that's a huge table,' she said.

The girl laughed as she took Miranda's hands in hers. 'You funny.... will you be mio amico ... my friend?'

The words tasted sweet. Miranda smiled and nodded. None of the girls at school had spoken to her with such uncomplicated candour.

'Rosa.' A woman waved from the front steps of the brown house.

'That's mia madre, my mother,' said the girl.

Miranda waved at the woman.

Rosa's mother beamed and spoke. Both girls laughed at the rapid burst of words.

When Miranda stepped onto the bus she saw the smiling face of Rosa. The two girls huddled together near the front. Bus trips to school became the favourite times for both girls.

On one trip, It was Miranda who held Rosa tight when the bus was slapped sideways. The world was silent, then crammed with screams and tearing of metal. She was allowed to visit Rosa in the hospital after the surgeons had saved the twisted fractured leg. No one could sooth Miranda's hiccupping grief. Not even Rosa's wan smiles penetrated her sadness. She hadn't known. She should have known. Nothing made sense. Where was the knowing when she needed it? It seemed the closer she was the less she knew. There were so many times when she knew useless things, hard things, illusive threads of things, smells, sounds. In the car on the way home she covered her ears, pushing away her mother's words of comfort. She refused dinner. She left the curtains open again that night and stared at the dark angry sky.

A few days later, after morning assembly, a new teacher stood at the front of the room. Her precious teacher, Miss Chambers was gone. No chance for goodbye. Her head ached. There was no air in the room. The new teacher kept asking if she was all right. She wasn't. She was solitary, helpless.

Miranda was the first to rush off the school bus. Rosa was home from hospital. Rosa's mother smiled, 'Come inside, little one. I have just made biscotti. Sit at the table.'

'Um ... okay.' Miranda sat on the edge of the high-backed chair. She looked around.

'Rosa is sleeping, but she will wake soon and be happy to see you. While we wait we will have my special cioccolata calda. Do you like chocolate? Of course, all children do.' Rosa's mother hummed as she worked.

Miranda felt her throat tighten. Her mother wouldn't be home until dusk. She quickly rubbed at her eyes to erase the sting of unexpected salty tears. 'Thank you,' she said, as she accepted the steaming mug. She was surprised when Rosa's mother sat down opposite her with her own mug and biscuit.

Come, little one, you must not be so sad. Rosa will be ... how you say? Good as new.' The woman regarded Miranda with searching brown eyes. 'Or is it something else?'

'My father is lost,' said Miranda, clattering the mug onto the table. She put her head down to hide her tears.

'Ah piccolo tesoro, this is what brings such sadness to one so young.' The woman swept Miranda into generous arms. 'Tell me all about it. What do you mean—lost?'

Miranda rested her head on the woman's shoulder and told of the past bleak years, of the sorrow that followed her like a shadow, of the questions. 'Daddy is a fisherman. Sometimes he is gone for months, but now they say he is lost at sea. But I don't understand. Grownups don't get lost. He has always come home before. Mother only says "I don't know". I can't ask her...'

'Of course, she is very sad too.'

'Oh ... yes.' Miranda frowned. She hadn't seen her mother cry, but had heard her wrenching sobs late into the night in those early months.

'You love him very much, your papà, and you miss him.' Rosa's mother wiped Miranda's eyes with the corner of her apron. 'Tell me about him, your papa.' It was a simple request, delivered with none of the fearful anxiety that surrounded all the previous conversations that tiptoed around the tragedy.

Miranda felt something break open inside. Words that had been dormant flowed, in awkward phrases and stammered sentences. Thoughts sprung to life in surprising bursts. She talked about Miss Chambers leaving. 'I couldn't say goodbye,' she sobbed.

Rosa's mother soothed her. 'But it is your papà you wish to say goodbye to, sì?'

Miranda's tears stopped. She wanted to scream 'No!' Saying goodbye to her father was unthinkable. She looked out the window. A tiny sparrow splashed in the birdbath under a laden fig tree. The tiny creature revelled in the act of dipping and bowing, wings fluttering.

'I ... I used to bring him luck, that's what he said. I always wound a piece of my hair around his finger before he left, but it didn't work. And now ... now I know things ... things that are going to happen ...'

'Ah, you mean chiaroveggenza, the special sight. You have this?' The woman looked deep into Miranda's eyes. 'But it makes you sad?'

Miranda nodded.

'Hmm,' said the woman. 'It is not something you ask for, this sight. Some say it is a gift, some not. But the goodbye, this is important. You will find a way, piccolo tresoro, to say goodbye to your precious papà when your heart is ready.'

The sun hovered, pinking the evening clouds. Miranda sat

on the old pier at the end of their block, where the land and water met. It was the first time she had been near the pier since her father had been declared Lost at Sea. For two long years she had hated the saltwater lake and the sea, but now ... Now it was the only connection with her father. She dipped her toes into the chill of the water and picked up a large round stone. She felt its smooth perfection, worn by centuries. Her father had told her that. Holding it in her palm, she rocked it up and down in a lilting rhythm, measuring its weight. It was what her father had done with his catch of perch or bream.

A dark-billed ibis sampling the last pickings of the day looked up when a grey flat frog croaked its discontent. The bird gave Miranda the impertinence of an indifferent stare before returning to her search for grubs by the shore.

Miranda threw the stone as far as she could into the moss-green crimpling of the lake. It disappeared with a timid splosh. Drawing her knees up to her chin, she put her head down and drew into herself. Her pale-blonde hair hung in tired tendrils as her heart cracked open like the clams her father flicked apart with strong brown hands. She could see him now, wiping sweat from his forehead with rolled up flannelette sleeves. Hot tears washed away the image that receded like the tide beneath her, with the water as old as time, the brine that knew every continent, every ocean and living thing in it. Then, far out to sea, water rose as vapour to the clouds and became rain, touching the earth, touching everything and everyone. Water knew the world as well as the people, like her father, who had fished its depths. It knew about heavy things, deep secrets, about the knowing.

When her tears were done with her, she reached into her pocket and took out a mud-rose velvet pouch. With grubby fingers she pulled out a tiny white feather, her father's last gift. With delicate care, she wound a strand of her hair around the shaft. When her father had given it to her, he told her it was a seagull's remige feather, a flight feather. The shadows had lengthened, reaching the rotting pier. Mother would be home soon. She would call to Miranda through the air as it became dense. The breeze grew stronger, dimpling the salt water.

Miranda sighed. She kissed the feather and held it high. The wind's breath caught it. The feather trembled, lifting gently at the sides. It ruffled, quivered into life, then took flight.

'Goodbye Daddy,' she whispered.

The feather drifted up in the air, then fluttered to the water. It floated for a moment, then dipped beneath the honeyed darkness, beginning its journey through the timeless waters to find her father.

Call me mate

Harry's place. The pub, his drinking mates – the ones he referred to as the usual crew. That was the world for Harry Blake. While his mates went home to other lives, when Harry left the pub, he left the only life he knew. His place. The only place he fit, if only for a few hours.

When he first moved into the mobile home in the village he'd thought, great, I'll have company. What a joke. All he heard were complaints. He was noisy when he came home. He didn't tend his 'bit of garden'. Naggers, the lot of them - bunch of busybodies. Probably counted the tally of long necks thrown in the bin. He'd taken to wrapping them in newspaper. He'd only had one friend, one mate in the village—old Bill Neighsmith. But even he had been picked up by his daughter and taken to live with her family. That stung.

He spent more time at the pub, trying to find more mates, daytime ones for when the usual crew were working. But that didn't work. He ended up drinking alone, wandering to the pokies, then off to the collect his welfare cheque.

He'd been important once. Served his country. Led a band of brothers into hell and back in Vietnam. There was no band of brothers now. Just a new hell.

And now, here he was drinking at home in front of the idiot box.

Harry Blake didn't hear the phone ring. He was suddenly transfixed by the television. Truth be told, not even his screaming ex-wife could have distracted him. And that was saying something. His hands trembled. He cursed himself for the fool he was. Every elocuted syllable from the voice of the journalist cut through him.

What had he been thinking when he casually mentioned to the guys over a few drinks that he'd seen some bloke climbing over the fence of the sports field on the night of the murder? For once they'd taken him seriously. Fred Gracken had solemnly said he should report it to the police. 'I'll go with ya, mate,' said Fred. 'Never know how useful these little things can be.'

Harry had never been called mate by the guys. The whole thing had snowballed from there. He could hardly refuse to assist with an identikit image.

He cringed as the police sketch flicked onto the screen. A stab of remorse grabbed his gut. He'd never been a liar. Acts of heroism were long over. He no longer concerned himself with exercising his conscience, but he'd committed no crimes.

But now, a nationwide search was under way. Every man and his dog were looking for George Benson – some poor sod who bore an uncanny resemblance to the police sketch he'd given. Harry wondered how he could ever tell anyone the man they sought was a figment of his random imaginings, born of a desire to belong to the crew, to be called mate again.

He turned the telly off.

Shadows

I

Prudence Wainwright adjusted her sunglasses. Normally she considered the wearing of sunglasses in a café as rather pretentious, but she wanted some peace and quiet, and at her age she could always plead sensitive eyes. Peace and quiet. It was unbelievable the number of people who came to her with gossip. For the life of her, she couldn't see why. Today she just wanted to read a magazine, have a frothy cappuccino, and watch the world go by. She'd had an early morning sherry to fortify herself for the day.

Thank God she didn't have to go to the school. Maybe she was getting too old for the school job. Being a casual receptionist for the school counsellor hadn't turned out as she expected.

It wasn't as if they needed the money. Earl was very successful as town planner. A valued member of the Council, he had just been elected Mayor. They were invited to all the best social engagements. It was a bit tiring at times, but one must do one's community duty.

It was a shame they hadn't had children. Earl had been disappointed; he would have made a good father. Prudence had worked hard over the years to fill the gap in every possible way. Earl hadn't been involved in the council youth programs so she felt that he surely didn't miss fatherhood. Their uncomplicated life allowed him to pursue his career and there was no denying that their status in the community was a boon. She was very proud of him. After all, everyone knew that behind every good man was a good woman. Their affluence, if one should call it that, did allow her some little indulgences to make up for his long hours and work commitments.

Originally glad to be out of the sun and humidity, Prudence was beginning to be bored. This was the best café in town, but honestly the service was slow. Today was her special day out. Every week she went all out on a hairdo and lunch. Normally she would have read a magazine or had a coffee before Adeline arrived, but today she was unaccountably tetchy.

What on earth was keeping Adeline? The one day she could do with some company and Addy was late. Not that Prudence called her that, she abhorred any abbreviations to names people were given. She looked at her watch. Adeline must have been caught up chatting to someone. That was the only drawback with her friend. She was a bit of a gossip, and Prudence was not in favour of that sort of thing.

Reaching for the menu for the hundredth time, Prudence consoled herself with the fact that she would feel so much better after her hair appointment. It gave her such a lift.

Looking out of the café window she saw a young woman with gorgeous red hair. Well, it would have been gorgeous if it had been tamed a little. But the colour, it was stunning. It was exactly the colour of Prudence's when she was young. She sighed. All the dye and pampering in the world had not managed to return her hair to its former glory.

Having nothing better to do, Prudence watched the girl. She seemed to be pouring over a map of some sort, occasionally looking up at the shops. Then she picked up a large woven basket with two long handles, not unlike a carpet bag, and crossed the road. She was heading for the café. A waiter jumped up to help her in the door. Oh dear, you could hardly see the girl for that wild mane.

'S'cuse me, Miss. I've been told a Mrs Prudence Wainwright is in this café. Could you please point her out if she's here?' The girl waved a grubby piece of paper.

Prudence blanched and sunk behind the menu. What on earth could this hippy person want with her? She hoped it wasn't a council matter. It was one of her pet hates when people seemed to hold her accountable for Earl's development decisions. Looking up, she was horrified to see the waitress directing the girl to her table.

'Look, my dear, if this is something to do with a council deci...' Prudence stopped dead. A carbon copy of her face at twenty was looking back at her. Except for those brown eyes...

'Ullo, Mum. I betcha never expected me to find you. It

was such a bloody struggle to get anywhere with that awful adoption agency woman. It was just real lucky for us that you arranged a private adoption, and I found that lovely old duck from the church that took care of it all. M'name's Willow now. Chose it m'self. ... Oh dear, are y'all right?'

Prudence heard a buzzing in her head.

The room spun. There was a strange voice penetrating the fuzziness.

'Quick, put her head down. She's going to faint.' Willow had lost her hippy voice and supported Prudence as she slumped to the floor.

A baby cried. The strange girl picked a tiny infant out of the carry all, and soothed it. The baby had no nappy. The basket was lined with an old towel.

'Shush, now, bub. Granny isn't well.'

'Granny?' It was Prudence Wainwright's last thought as everything went black.

She was later heard to say that there was a beautiful light in the distance, beckoning her. It wouldn't do for anyone to think that she, Prudence Wainwright, had missed out on an 'other-worldly' experience. Why they might think she was without redemption.

While the world stopped then for the unconscious Prudence Wainwright, chaos reigned around her. An ambulance was called. A crowd gathered.

Willow Brown, Prudence's visitor, and newly discovered daughter, organised the crowd with calm self-assurance. No one dared argue with this confident carbon-copy of Prudence. Her lineage was accepted without question.

Someone phoned Earl's secretary and informed him of what had happened. A temp covering for Earl's long-time assistant, the new girl calmly accepted the presence of a daughter in her boss's life. After all, he was an intensely private man and she hadn't had time for office gossip, she'd been too busy working out the basics of her job and too nervous to ask the other staff for information. She noticed the colour drain from his face at the news. Then, grabbing his coat, he rushed out of the office without a word.

Another office worker, tapped into the local grapevine, and sensing a monetary reward from the newspapers, phoned and tipped them off, so that when Earl arrived at the local public hospital, cameras were flashing from all directions outside the Accident and Emergency Ward.

On arrival at the A & E, Earl was confronted by a strange girl who was the image of Prudence around the time he met her. This garrulous new person had already gained validity as Prudence's only child, and was holding court with the press. She gave a detailed account of the terrible health crisis of her newly-found mother, adding a gentle sniff and a well-timed tear or two.

Earl's customary presence of mind completely deserted him in the face of such inexplicable circumstances. All he could do was stutter.

When the basket Willow was carrying let out a loud howl, the staff were shocked, as she had travelled in the ambulance to the hospital. The infant hadn't been restrained. The A&E supervisor cornered the ambulance driver, a paramedic.

The paramedic couldn't remember being more embarrassed when he was asked by a gathering of journalists why he'd done something so reckless and against the law. The explanation that he thought the young woman merely had a rather large tatty carryall didn't seem adequate, so with his best authoritative voice he said, 'Step aside, will you lot! There's a very ill woman here.'

The supervisor decided that discretion was indeed the better part of valour. With a growing audience he stepped in to part the crowd of journalists to allow the ambulance men to push the trolley with an unconscious Prudence Wainwright through the patient entrance. Then he ushered Earl and Willow through the glass doors to the Accident and Emergency waiting room, where a burly hospital security man had been hastily called to guard the door.

II

In the cubicle next to Prudence Wainwright, Byron Galloway, overdose victim and alcohol poisoning patient in Bed 4, made a conscious effort to relax, as the nurse organising his transfer to the ward swished the curtain across in a vain attempt at privacy for the new admission.

After being in the emergency room for 10 hours the worst of Byron's hallucinations were over, although things were still a bit hazy. The place was pandemonium, staff bustling everywhere. Some old duck had had "an event". Some politician's wife, he'd gathered that much—he'd overheard "mayor". The woman was getting instant attention. Two nurses were asking questions and discussing obs, as machines were wheeled in and out. Through the gap in the curtain he saw a different doctor to the one he'd had, attending to the woman and giving the nurses permission to let family in.

Then the old bird's husband arrived. He was followed by a weird orange-haired hippy woman with a squalling baby, who was asked to sit in the waiting area. She protested like mad, saying she was the woman's daughter. The noise level went through the roof. It was a right circus. Byron strained to see, but it was all a blur of activity. Staff were running round like mad, ranting about the media. Lots of media, apparently. Even though they were in the waiting area their presence could be heard.

Byron was alert then. If he hadn't been a patient himself the whole thing would have amused him. Apparently the old bird had adopted a kid out a thousand years ago—must be the orange-haired hippy. So Mr VIP Mayor, had arrived to discover that not only was his wife on the brink of death, she had a secret daughter, and a grandkid. That conversation had been very enlightening. The hippy woman was a loud piece of work. The staff and ambos hadn't been impressed, and God only knows what the VIP made of it all. Someone would have their work cut out to put a positive spin on this lot. Byron bristled at the unfairness of it all. The politician would come out of it squeaky clean. They got all the breaks, and he'd be treated like a criminal.

He heard the name Prudence Wainwright. Byron knew her. Everyone in Noarlunga knew Mayor Wainwright's busybody wife. He'd even been cornered by her a few times himself. He shuddered at the thought. The nurses thought they were whispering, assuming he was too far gone to understand. He smirked as he was wheeled away from the chaos to the ward.

He was shocked to be put in a four-bed women's ward, but was too grateful for the sedative he was given to offset the effects of the alcohol in his system to care.

Byron felt a light touch on his shoulder. A headless Benji weaved around the room, blood spurting. There was a dark shadow following him. It must be the grim reaper, come for him.

He shuddered awake. He must have drifted off. Shit, what a nightmare. Thank goodness he didn't have reactions like that all the time. He'd give the stuff up in a heartbeat. He remembered a friend's saying about hash. 'It's like a good looking woman who doesn't have to offer you anything. You know you want her. You know she'll break your balls and suck the soul right out of you; but you still want to have her.'

The mother of all headaches was cracking his skull open. His stomach felt like he had been stampeded by a herd of elephants, from the numerous hurling episodes of last night. He must have been ripped out of his mind.

With only a thin curtain between them, the crackling wheeze from the patient in the next bed sounded like a car backfiring. If that old bag made that whistling bloody noise again Byron would go and kill her himself. So, she was dying. So what! Everyone died. Everything had a beginning and an end. It was her time to go, that's all. Why the hell was she in this fucking last place in earth you wanted to be, hospital ward? Weren't there hospices for this sort of thing?

One thing was certain—this wasn't going to happen to him again. You had to make a mistake to learn from it and he was no idiot. He'd never buy his stash from that lowlife, pisshead Benji again. What sort of a fucked up name was Benji anyway. But even as he vowed to ditch Benji, the memory of the hash in his gym bag at the house made him nervous. He was playing for higher stakes now–selling small amounts to friends he trusted. He shuddered as he wondered if anyone else had found the latest stuff a bit strong.

Shit, that was the only part of this whole business he hated. The insecurity of the quality of the gear. They should get it right, the dickheads. He laughed ironically at his own train of thought. Quality Control, Occupation Health & Safety courses for dealers. Yeah right!

Not that he thought of Benji as a 'dealer'–he was a supplier. A supplier of a service that was just misunderstood. Illegal and misunderstood. It made him angry. Especially now that he had a few kilos stashed at the old man's house. He would never call that place home. He should have been in a condo on the beach by now, would have if he hadn't lost his job. His boss had tossed him like a piece of garbage. So he'd had a bad month, everyone in sales had those. He'd tried to explain that he was stuck with his old man who was really ill, but Dave didn't buy it. Guess everyone in this town knew his father was a good-for-nothing drunk.

Byron would not have admitted, even to himself that he'd started smoking in the morning, at lunch time and again at the end of every day. To keep him calm. To get to sleep. To get him through to the next day. It was no different than going to the doc to get something to help him calm down, chill out.

Why did government health authorities ban something that had less evidence of harm than tobacco smoking? Why hell, if they would come out of the closet and tell him just what their story was, show the compelling body of indisputable evidence that put marijuana off the legal list, why he'd be the first to believe and give it up.

They hadn't banned tobacco even though they paid huge bucks to advertise its harmful effects. If it was as bad as they said it was then why didn't they get off their collective legislating arses and outlaw it, arrest people and be done with it? Put their money where their mouth was. That was probably what it all came down to anyway, money.

The wheeze in the next bed turned into a rattle that echoed on every side of his skull. Jesus, he couldn't take much more of this.

'Sorry, Son,' said a feeble voice. Oh shit, he must have said it out loud. He pushed the pillow around his ears and groaned. Oh shit. For the first time in that interminable day he felt sorry for someone other than himself. Poor silly old bitch wasn't dying just to annoy him.

'Didn't mean to be rude, lady,' he grumbled reluctantly. 'I just have a headache that would split concrete and I've hurled all night.'

'That's dreadful,' responded the voice behind the curtain. 'Why don't you ring the nurse and ask for something? Can I help?'

Oh Jeez, sympathy from the dying now. This had to be his worst day on earth.

'Yeah well,' he said with a half-hearted chuckle, 'they aren't likely to do that as my present problem came about because of a little too much medication already, if you get my drift.'

'Oh, I see, you hit the bottle and it hit you back.' Her voice was so soft he could hardly catch what she was saying.

'Something like that,' he said dismissively. He rolled over noisily, making the hospital bed squeak, hoping she would take the hint.

She didn't speak again. Well, maybe she was dead. He suddenly thought how horrible it would be to be a few feet away from someone when they died. Jeez, get me out of here, he thought. Then the crackling wheeze began again and he breathed a sigh of relief.

The nurse came in. It was the skinny blonde with the big laugh. Melda or Melody or something. She'd introduced herself to the two of them a few hours ago. Chatted away like a bloody cheerful parrot she had. What sort of people were nurses anyway? Walking into rooms with people taking their last breath, and idiots like him who had accidentally overdosed, and treating them as if they were all at some god-dammed Wiggles concert.

The nurse flicked the curtain back with a swoosh. The metal curtain rings sounded like screaming metal. He moaned.

'Is your head still bad,' she said sympathetically. 'Do you want me to get you something for it?'

'Didn't think I could have anything,' he muttered. 'Thought you people didn't give dope addicts anything? You think we deserve our suffering for being fucking idiots.'

'Slight paranoia creeping in, Byron. Are you a dope addict?' she asked, with a teasing smile. She tilted her head to the side as she looked at him. Wow! She was a stunner up close.

'No, I'm not,' he denied defensively.

'Never touch the stuff, huh?' she folded her arms across the nursing notes on the plastic clipboard. God he wished she would stop talking and trying to make him think. His head pounded.

'I didn't say that. I know what you lot think but there is a huge difference between a dope addict and a recreational user.'

Byron sat up in the bed to lessen the feeling that the girl had a towering advantage over him. He felt a bit overwhelmed by this cool, good-looking chick. He must look like the bottom of a fish bowl.

'Ah, so you're a fucking idiot.' She held his gaze. 'Your words, not mine.'

'Oh, so that's my official diagnosis, is it nurse?' He was angry now.

'It's like this Byron. There is a huge difference between the official diagnosis and the real diagnosis.'

'You're pretty uptight about it. You nurses like the stuff as much as the rest of us. I've seen plenty of you smoking weed.'

'Sounds like you have quite a body of evidence for an occasional user,' she mocked.

'Yeah well,' he spat out, 'more evidence that you medical fucking experts can come up with.' He snorted, realising that he was making a poor show of himself. He wished she would go away, she was better to look at than to listen to.

She laughed. 'I'll bring you something as soon as I've given Helena her nebuliser.'

'That's what they all say,' he whined.

What was it with her? She was still cheerful, while he felt so wound up he could spit nails. With deft expert hands she undid the tubing of the nebulizer and filled the small receptacle on the mask with a plastic ampoule from a metal tray. He was in awe at her ease with it all. How good would it be if you could get your gear that easily. Just line up for it. No phone calls, no sly meetings avoiding cops or prying eyes. There'd be no relying on mates or dodgy idiots, who acted like they'd known you forever merely because you shared a laugh over a spliff, and they claimed to know where to get the best hash.

He sunk back into the bed, suddenly exhausted from the mental effort of talking. Grateful that the nurse had pulled the curtain, Byron tried to relax. At least the thin curtain might stop the woman in the bed next to him from yakking. It had discomforted him no end when she'd casually mentioned that her husband was a private investigator.

Just as he thought he might actually drift off, the woman had visitors. Two teenage girls. Through the gap in the curtain he saw that one of them was a blonde piece he'd chatted up on the train. The one who'd pretended to be deaf and humiliated him. Byron froze. The blonde was the daughter of the local private investigator. It wasn't exactly a connection to the cops, but it was too close for comfort. Life was certainly conspiring against him. He turned over slowly and pulled the sheet above his head.

Paranoia set in as Byron thought of his stash. It was safer in his wardrobe at his father's rundown place. The old dude might be a useless drunk but he sure knew how to send the cops packing.

There was silence in the room. The girls had gone.

Where was that nurse with his pain relief? He'd never needed anything more.

He couldn't wait to be out of the place. He would have signed himself out, but that would gain more attention. He'd just be quiet and polite. Benji was the only one who knew about his stash and not even he knew where it was hidden. He was safe. He couldn't let paranoia get the better of him.

The wheeze from the woman had eased. There was now the whirr of a nebuliser machine. At least she had peace. Even Byron, in his selfish state of mind, could wish her that. The whoosh of the mist she was sucking in seemed as precious as God's own breath, straight to her.

Byron wondered briefly what had happened to the Mayor's wife, busybody Mrs Wainwright. She'd been in the A&E ward next to him. With a secret daughter, and a screeching baby. Ha. There was some justice in life. Mr Mayor had scandal on his own door now.

Welcome to the real world, Grandpa. And as for Mrs Gossip Wainwright—Granny!

III

The object of Byron's musings was in a private room on the general ward. While she should have been grateful the transfer from the busy A&E, Prudence Wainwright was engaged with musings of her own. Assisted with a hefty dose of morphine she abandoned her stiff persona and wandered lightly back into the past.

As soon as she'd looked beyond the likeness of her younger self in her daughter, she had seen the rich brown eyes of an American soldier who'd served in Vietnam. What a beautiful man he'd been—Willow's father. Wounded inside and out, Chuck Reise had awakened a powerful longing in Prudence. For the first time in her life she was needed, desired. She set out to heal his suffering in the age-old manner of besotted women the world over; in bed. Or was it a bunk–isn't that what he'd called the tiny bench on the ship where he'd taken her willingly offered virginity?

Apparently it had healed him, she thought, with not a small measure of bitterness, for he was gone in days; with not a word or a backward glance. But he had left something behind. A child.

The one gift she'd been unable to give to dear Earl, who would have made the best of fathers. Earl, the meticulous man who noticed her quiet reserve in the solicitor's office where she had worked. All those years ago.

To all appearances Prudence had managed to reinvent herself after the birth of the child and the adoption. When she gained a position at a prestigious law firm she had forbidden any shortening of her name. The Prue of the past was gone. Her floral prints were replaced with stern suits, with just a modest cowl neck to soften the look. She wore her hair up, coiled tightly in a barrette. Not a wisp was allowed to stray. She would never be a plaything again.

Earl had been a fresh-faced junior partner in those days. He was five years younger than her—just a 'pup'. Beside him, she felt jaded and wounded. Until he asked her out.

He'd been persistent in those days–intrigued by her. The shadow of sorrow she wore translated as something else, something he wanted. Prudence Drago had never been pursued–she'd been needed and yes, desired, but not sought after like a prize. He never looked at the office beauties with their carefree party lifestyles. He wanted her. She'd intended to tell him about the child, the hasty adoption her mother had organised, but things had moved so quickly. Before she had even formed her own feelings, Earl had gone down on one knee.

The right time had never come.

Hot tears scalded her eyes and she blinked them back. She would not cry, not now. But dear God, what would she lose? Everything she had so patiently worked for? Her husband? Her home? It didn't bear thinking about, but there it was— gnawing at her like an abscessed tooth.

She loved Earl. Not with the desperate passion that had swept her away in her youth with the American, but with friendship, warmth and gratitude. She determined to become everything she thought he wanted, charting an ambitious course to status. At first it had been for Earl, but somewhere along the way it had become about her. She was a valued asset, a woman of substance. How often she'd prided herself on achieving the precise life she'd always wanted, a life far from her humble roots. But now, in one fell swoop, all of that was in jeopardy, unravelling before her eyes.

If only the meeting with her daughter hadn't been so public. If only she hadn't taken a turn and ended up the centre of a media circus. If only she hadn't allowed her mother to arrange a private adoption; expedient at the time. This one factor made the way clear for her daughter to find her.

If only she'd had time to prepare Earl. Dear Earl. How would he react? He had brought security and reliability into her life. He'd given her the dream life she had striven so hard to attain. Earl had been so grateful when she'd welcomed their relocation from the city to Noarlunga, never knowing her relief that the move would distance her even further from the past. A new town had delivered the safety she craved, and with Earl's involvement in the community and rise to prominence in the council, she'd become a real part of the place.

In an instant her world had tilted. It was too late to go back. It was impossible to go forward. While the baby she'd only glanced at in the delivery room remained a shadowy figure in the past, she had almost been able to convince herself that none of it had happened.

But now that shadow was real.

*From *Shadow Girl*

Who

'Quite a five o'clock shadow you have there, Brady.' Jim Harcourt raised a hand to block out the sun, as he assessed his son. 'I nearly mistook you for a removalist. You could've come and got me to help. I'm only next door.'

'The removalists came a few days ago.' Brady tugged at his beard self-consciously. 'It's not staying.'

'Who's not staying?' Betty tugged on Jim's arm.

'I must have been out when they came. You right Bett?'

'Did you check the mail, Jim?' Betty looked up to her husband.

'It's Sunday Bett.' Jim frowned as Betty bent down and tugged at weeds beside the path. 'How's the unpacking going son?'

'Well on the way, Dad.'

'Your lights were on till all hours. You could've asked for help. A man likes to feel useful, son. Especially to his own.'

Brady shrugged. 'Nice to see you too, Dad.'

'Hello, Grandie. Hi Gran.' Ebony giggled, hugging her

grandfather warmly while Betty smiled absently. 'How do you like Dad's beard? He's aiming for Soho Hippy.'

'Well he missed. He'd frighten the dead,' said Jim whisking Ebony into his arms. 'How are you settling in poppet?'

Brady sighed. 'We were just leaving for a walk on the beach. Then have lunch at the kiosk.'

'Oh, how lovely. A walk along the beach. What a wonderful idea,' said Betty. 'Did you bring my hat, Jim?'

Brady swallowed his frustration. Plans for time with his daughter were being derailed. He threw his father a beseeching look, but Jim was watching Betty like a hawk. 'Sure, we could all go.'

'Yes, Betty. It's in the car with the golf bag.'

'Oh Jim, you know I hate golf,' Betty pouted, crossing her arms in childlike defiance.

'I wasn't going to play golf, Bett,' said Jim.

'Why can't you play golf Grandie? I'll come with you,' said Ebony. 'Dad can take Gran to the beach.' She ran inside and came back with her iPod. Linking her arm through her grandfather's, she smiled at her father. 'You don't mind, do you, Dad.'

'He'd love it,' said Jim. 'I'll fetch your mother's hat and bag.'

As Brady walked with his mother along the track leading to the beach he could have sworn he heard Ebony say, 'Thanks Grandie, I needed rescuing from Dadzilla today.'

At the beach the only sounds that intruded were the rhythmic flapping of the umbrellas over the outdoor dining area, the distant caw caw of the seagulls with the soft slapping of the ocean on the shore in the background.

Brady and his mother sat on the whitewashed benches that faced the ocean. The sea carelessly lapped the bleached sand. The scene before them was idyllic, but it failed to bring the calm Brady desperately needed.

Moving into the cottage that overlooked the craggy cliffs had kept father and daughter busy. Unpacking and sorting provided Brady with a sense of control. Unfortunately it proved to be short-lived. He'd been unprepared for Ebony's outburst over the photos. How could he explain that the woman in the photos was a reminder of the young woman who disappeared into another world? The unpredictable world of her mental illness. It wasn't even grief that made the photos unbearable, it was the sense he should have been able to do something. Make her keep taking her medication; something, anything.

Betty was the picture of contentment as she licked her ice cream. Try as he might, Brady couldn't remember his mother ever having an ice cream. She was in her own world, she'd hardly said a word to him on the walk there.

The quiet was shattered by the laughing voices of a woman and child. They were roller-blading, hands entwined. The boy, who was about seven or eight, was concentrating so hard he gnawed his bottom lip. Wearing enough protective gear to start their own shop, they were different, but strangely in sync. The woman's movements were effortless, but she took great care to pace herself to the boy who was clearly struggling. She wore purple leggings and a bright multi-coloured mini skirt that swayed rhythmically as she moved, the colours of a gypsy, colours Scarlett would have worn. Brady's jaw clenched.

'I think that's enough for now Dylan,' said the woman gently, her voice a combination of richness and warmth. Taking off their helmets they sat at a nearby table.

'Will I ever be as good as you, Emma?' asked the boy, gazing up at the woman with innocent adoration.

'Of course you will,' she said, reaching down and massaging the boy's calf muscles. 'When your leg heals I won't be able to keep up with you.'

Looking away, Brady stared at the horizon, pushing back the image of the newcomer. Her tenderness to the boy had stirred a distant memory. Of a time when Scarlett was young and carefree, a time when he was the centre of her world, and the light of his daughter's days. He remembered how Ebony smothered him with kisses and begged for horsey rides on his back as soon as he walked through the door. How he longed to recapture those moments. He might have lost Scarlett, but he'd be damned if he was going to lose Ebony.

Brady dragged his attention back to the last of his ice-cream. He'd forgotten about it and sticky liquid was dribbling down his hand. His mother handed him a lace handkerchief. Really! She'd be wiping his face next.

The morning crowd was growing. A mother with a baby in a pram and a toddler had arrived noisily. The toddler began to chase the seagulls, shrieking with delight as they took to the air.

'There goes the neighbourhood,' muttered Brady. His

mother stared at him and moved her chair away from him.

The woman looked up. She took off her sunglass and waved to Betty. 'Hello Betty, how are you? I hope you're not going surfing. You'll get your dressing wet. We have to look after that ulcer if it's going to heal properly.'

'Oh Emma, you're such a trick. As if I could ever surf! Couldn't do much more than dogpaddle, dear.' Betty rose and walked towards the two. 'May I sit here?'

'Of course, Betty. You're welcome,' said Emma. 'That's quite an ice-cream you have there.'

'That young man bought it for me.' She waved a nonchalant hand in Brady's direction.

Brady stilled with shock. *That young man*? Had he misheard? What was wrong with his mother? She hadn't said a word on the walk there.

Emma reached down and checked Betty's leg. There was a large dressing on her shin. Brady couldn't believe he hadn't noticed it before. 'Looking good, Betty. Jim's taking good care of you then.'

Betty beamed.

A one legged gull hopped to the table near the boy. Betty bent down. Holding a small piece of her ice cream cone she reached towards the bird. Delicately it took the morsel from her hand and gulped it hungrily.

'Wow, how'd you do that? That's so cool. I wish it would take food from my hand.'

'You have to hold your hand very still,' said Betty. Smiling at the boy she repeated the gesture. They were soon lost in their own world, chattering with ease. The gull took food from the boy's hand. 'It's not fair; this bird only has one leg and can't get around like the others.'

'Until he flies. He'll be all right then. You'll see,' said Betty, 'you watch. Fly birdie, fly,' Betty waving at the gull. In a sudden rush of white wings the gull took to the air effortlessly.

'You're right! He did it!' The boy looked down at his own leg.

'Do you have a bad leg too?' asked Betty.

'Yes. I was in a really bad car accident and broke my leg in three places. But I'm getting better. I had a whole leg plaster up to here for two months, and dressings as well. I have a scar. See? Mum says it looks like a half moon, but I think it looks like lightning.' He turned his leg for Betty to have a better look.

'Definitely lightning,' she responded. The boy smiled and returned to his chips.

Betty leaned in close to the blonde and whispered. Emma shot Brady a look of mild alarm and patted her hand. Betty gripped the woman's arm. Brady attempted a smile. It must have been a poor effort because the blonde's eyes clouded. Betty's whispering grew more intense.

Brady rose and went over to their table, extending his hand to Emma. 'Hello, I'm...'

Betty burst into tears and threw herself at the woman. 'Make him go away. He's a stranger. He's been following me all day.'

'I don't believe this!' Brady threw his hands heavenward.

'I think you'd better step back, sir,' said Emma. 'I don't know who you are, but you're upsetting my client.'

'Your *"client"*? Oh, that's rich,' muttered Brady. 'Listen lady...'

Betty clutched at Emma's sleeve. 'Take me home, Emma. *Please.* Jim will be worried. I don't like this man.'

Brady took a step closer and Betty's sobs grew louder. Brady's jaw dropped. Emma rose decisively. Linking her arm through Betty's she beckoned to the boy, who was now also looking worried.

'Oh, for crying out loud,' Brady said, reaching for his wallet. Unbelievable. He would actually have to show this woman his ID. He fumbled with the wallet. 'Wait a minute...ah, Miss...'

'Look, sir. It doesn't really matter right now who you are. Right or wrong, Betty's upset. I am her nurse.' Emma pointed to the badge on her shirt. 'I see her twice a week. The best thing we can do right now is for me to take her home to familiar surroundings. The best thing you can do is step aside and work this out later, okay.'

Before Brady could utter another word, the trio walked quickly across the road to a white hatchback with Noarlunga Community Nursing scripted on the side. 'Bloody hell!' Brady slumped back onto the bench.

An old man sitting nearby dragged himself stiffly out of his chair, then giving Brady a wide berth, shuffled as quickly as he could across the road.

Retrieving his mobile from his pocket, Brady quickly punched in his father's number. He'd have to interrupt Jim's game of golf and tell him to return home. It wouldn't do for his mother to arrive home to an empty house. He'd never hear the end of this. The mobile displayed one bar.

Out of service. Thrusting the mobile back into his pocket, he cursed out loud.

Brady was shaken by his mother's reaction. She'd always seemed fine on the phone. What had just happened? Had his mother really not known him?

A tap on his shoulder startled him out of his reverie.

'Excuse me, sir, but I would like you to accompany me to the station to answer a few questions,' said a stern looking policeman.

From Scarlett doesn't live here anymore.

Too Deep, too soft, too alive

Too Deep

I am drowning, fighting, screaming for the surface. Kicking the dark aside. Fleeing the sucking depths that drag at my feet. My lungs cramp, pain and pressure sears. I swallow, and keep swallowing. The world is indigo, fathomless and foreign, and I am its prey.

Something's caught in my throat, filling my gullet, expanding, tearing. It pushes at my tongue, probing. I gag. My stomach fills, rejects, explodes. I hurl fiery liquid that burns like a naked flame.

My arm is gripped, squeezed. I want to open my eyes, but I don't want the water to burn them too. A woman's voice moans. Is someone else drowning too? Is it me? Clanging metal scrapes my eardrums. I hear a slap and the back of my hand smarts. Then, the pinch of a needle sting. Then calm. I sigh. Open one eye. A gloved hand draws blood into a syringe.

I'm dreaming. Water sloshes rhythmically near my ear. The vein in my arm chills. I hear seagulls, or voices. I no longer know my senses. I'm rocked by the murmur of ocean waves.

Without warning my body thrashes. Every muscle jerks, wrenches. I can't control anything. My head connects with a metal bar.

The seagulls are screeching now. I'm thrown on my side. I taste the rusty tang of fear, and know it is my own before the darkness reaches out and sucks me under.

Too soft

I am neither awake, nor asleep. I hear soft footsteps on velvet, the whisper of early morning secrets. Even the whoosh-slump-burr sound near me is softer than a newborn's lips.

I'm held tight. I strain. Am I in a shroud? Is it too late? Too late to live. I want to scream and rave, claw at the sky. I don't want to be dead, be gone. Not before I've even tried. Because I haven't. Tried. Through thin slits of stinging, reluctant eyes, I see dim light, rows of lights, soft orbs, neatly aligned. They blur and pulse.

Like a battered fish being jerked from the sea, I rise through a thousand swift levels of consciousness until my body's throbbing ache rouses me completely. My cramped hands search around me. Thin tubing is wrapped around my arm, but when I grab it, pain stabs my hand. I force my eyes open. It's an intravenous drip.

My face is wet. I've dribbled on a stiff, white pillow. There are metal bars, bedrails. I peer through them. They frame a pair of white shoes. I smell the sharp, sweet tang of Lynx, like my father used to wear. The memory bruises, jars my breathing into gasps and sobs.

I turn away. There's a raw burning in my throat as I try to form words. Agony grips my muscles. I hug myself and groan.

'That's the seizures, love, hell on y'muscles.' A mellow voice, soft and low. 'Your first time?' it asks.

I gargle a raw sound. 'Wha...?'

'Your first overdose?'

Too alive

I am at the edge of myself. I am all edge and only edge. My only existence is epidermal. I am hollow, gouged out of myself. I am skin, and only skin. Every nerve, thought and perception is at the edge of me. I am the edge.

There's a needle in my vein. Nothing new there. I am expert at vein-finding, venepuncture. But this needle is attached to a floppy fish-like bag with the impressive title of Normal Saline, along with other obscure elements of the periodic table, listed in minute print. Too small for my punctured eyes to read.

I am too alive. Much too undead. So far from my mediocre neutrality I cringe. A thousand ants crawl on my skin, not biting, and not entirely unpleasant, but so deeply unfamiliar that I'm afraid. I'm afraid of this skin-feeling, this aliveness. It's not what I expected. I expected spasming agony & disconnect, screaming rebellion at my loss, the defection and abandonment of my desire, my mistress, Heroin.

Not this, this hyper-awareness of being. It's not what I thought, this purging, this detoxification in this too bright white place. On my too small hospital bed that threatens to shudder and throw me off, turn me out.

The breeze burns. I know it's only gentle—the others turn smiling faces towards it, those normal ones, the ones who've never attempted the monstrous escape from themselves that I have perfected.

It's strange to think that this process of peeling away the numbness of self, the reluctant quest to rediscover an internal me should require such a carving out, hollowing—

remaking from the edges.

He said I died, there, alone, the paramedic who bruised my sternum, cracked a rib bringing me back. A man kinder than any other. But. Now. I am too alive.

Coastlines 7, Southern Cross University anthology

The boarding house

The vegetable truck lurches to a stop on the kerb outside 84 Henry Street, Quirindi, a two-storey Old Colonial, once the grandest domicile in the street, but more lately a boarding house, presided over by the widowed Ethel Ennis, a stout woman with firm jaw and fine white hair, restrained with meticulous care in a bun at the back of her head.

The driver parps the horn three times, leaps out and throws the canvas flaps back.

Inside the house, Ethel is listening to ABC radio and shouts 'Bravo!' at the news that mass immunisation for polio will begin. Not in time for her sister Bea's dragging leg but good news for others nonetheless.

Ethel's granddaughter, nine-year-old Lucy, sits on the front verandah, toes pressed together, pink ballet shoes tapping an impatient rhythm. When her grandmother fails to respond to the lure of the vegetable truck, she calls through the open kitchen window. 'Nanna! It's Mr Evans. Come get strawberries!'

The vegetable truck moves on. Lucy sighs and wriggles back in the seat. There's no use nagging Nanna Ennis for anything.

Clouds puff across the sky. Spring rain falls in soft warm splatters, trembling on amber-spiked florets of the grevilleas that edge the house.

Lucy shivers, causing a braid of copper-red hair to loosen its spiralled confinement. 'Bother,' she says, smoothing the tangle, 'Dad took ages platting my hair.'

An open magazine flutters in the breeze, its pages displaying a range of birthday cakes.

A large white hen is perched on the child's lap, as composed as any queen on a throne. 'I'll be ten-years-old soon, Esmeralda.' Lucy whispers, as if birthdays are secrets, kept only by regal white hens with magic powers, or if speaking aloud about birthdays will somehow lead to their disappearance.

Nine-year-old Lucy Meredith Carter is acquainted with acts of disappearance.

Leaving her seat, Lucy wanders to the back yard, hoping to find the returned digger, the only one of Nanna's boarders who is always there and ready for a chat.

The digger sees Lucy's hastily discarded bike on the ground picks it up and rests it against a nearby tree. It's hard to believe four years have passed since his arrival at the boarding house on a darker, forbidding day, back in '51, the year of the Commonwealth Jubilee.

Henry Street, QUIRINDI, 1951

Negligent clouds crept across the sun, then continued on their way in a sullen sky. Light filtered through cast-iron lacework, mottled the front verandah of the old house in a parade of shifting shadows that flashed and leapt like dark, slender ghosts.

Heavy velvet drapes, pushed aside partway, allowed pale autumn sunlight but faint presence in the front room—a former reception area, filled with guests, dark-clad and solemn, whose stilted conversation, constant checking of timepieces, and glances at the front door suggested a desire to be elsewhere.

An obligation to their hostess, implied by a table laden with food held them captive as they murmured softly phrased condolences and sympathies.

Huddled in a dim corner sat a small girl whose copper-red hair provided the only colour in the dull room. She tugged at a dark, oversized dress that hung to her ankles, chafing at the heavy fabric.

The dress, borrowed from a distant cousin, never met, had been handed to her that morning by her bustling grandmother, Ethel, who reigned with stoic dignity over a wake for her daughter, the child's mother. The child stared at a faded Persian rug, shrinking from her grandmother's pleas to eat or drink. Seeing curious eyes on her, she ran outside. Throwing herself on a hay bale, she sobbed.

A large white hen wandered near, hopped onto the bale, neck tilted, one sharp, black eye fixed on the girl as it pranced closer.

Curving the bird into her arms the child fell asleep. Unfazed by the child's twitching dreams, the hen tucked its head under a wing.

A soldier sat on the bottom rung of the thick timber steps at the far end of the verandah whittling a stick he found lying around. His digger's hat was pushed back. Tamed and slicked hair—inky black.

When the child woke, she rubbed swollen, sleepy eyes, then, still cradling the hen she wandered over to the soldier.

'Hello,' she said. 'Who are you?'

'I'm Harry.' The soldier paused to flick wood shavings from his knee.

'My name is Lucy Meredith Carter. You must be a new boarder. Have you been here long?'

'I arrived today.' Harry pointed at the kit bag resting at his feet.

'I'm s'posed to call grownups uncle or auntie, for respect. Can I call you Uncle Harry?'

'Sure. That'll be just fine.'

'This is my Nanna's boarding house.' The child waved an outstretched arm, as if to include the known universe, then kissed the tolerant bird on the head. 'Nanna's a bit bossy, but I 'spec you're used to that, being in the army and all.'

'I'm sure I'll manage, child.'

I'm bezactly five and a half.' She held up five fingers, a

feat made difficult by the wriggling hen under her arm. 'This is my chook, she's magic. She magicked herself to me. Most likely she thinks I'm her chick.'

'I see,' said Harry, 'how marvellous.'

He watched the child gnaw her bottom lip with tiny white teeth, heard her sigh.

'She's not zactly a pet. She's acshally Nanna Ennis' chook. I'll have to ask Dad if I can take her home. But I'm sure he'll let me, speshally when he knows she's magic.

Lucy nodded her head up and down. 'You'll see.'

'If you say so, missy. You'd better give her a name then.'

The child pushed a chubby finger into her cheek and looked up at the sky. 'Hmm. a magic chook should have an extra special name. Do you know any good names, Uncle Harry? I bet you've read a bunch of books. Old people usually have.'

The child had translucent skin with a smattering of freckles. Startling green eyes watched Harry.

The hen stared at him as if she too was waiting.

'What about Esmeralda?' Harry said.

'Ooh, I like that. It's a lovely name.

Where's it from?'

'A very old book—*The Hunchback of Notre Dame* ... erm, Esmeralda was a gypsy who lived in Paris a long time ago. She rescued a poor misshapen man by claiming sanctuary for him in a cathedral.'

A frown wrinkled Lucy's forehead.

Harry banged his head with a hand—he was making a hash of it. He hadn't had much to do with kids.

'What's sancsharry?' she brushed tangled curls from her

face with a casual backhanded swipe.

'Well. Er ... She hid him in a church.'

'Oh. Did she use magic?'

'I don't think so. Esmeralda was just very brave, but that's a kind of magic.'

The child's eyes filled with disappointment.

'People keep telling me to be brave.' She jerked at a rumble of noise from the house. 'There's lots of people here today. My mum Sylvia died and had a fun'ral.'

'Lucy!' Her father stood at the top of the stairs, eyes taut with worry.

Tucking the hen under her chin she stepped lightly up the wooden stairs and slipped her hand into her father's. 'I'm here, Dad.' She held up the hen with pleading eyes. The bird clucked with indignation at the movement.

'This is my new pet chook, Dad. Her name's Esmeralda and she's magic. She's helping me be brave.'

His answer was a soft low murmur. She listened with a tired smile then put her cheek on his hand, looking up at him with such tender admiration that Harry's heart tripped.

It was an image that reminded him of his own mother's fear in those fatherless days in London during the Great War.

LONDON, 1916

'I need you to be brave, Harry.' My mother pulled her coat around her over her nightgown as we hurried for the door. I was six years old. The war had been going on for half my life.

The country was in blackout every night. Air-raid sirens were nothing new, but there'd only been one bombing of London by a German Zeppelin, on the other side of the city. At school, we boys talked about the Zepps with excitement. The war was far away and more of an adventure than anything else. However, my mother, like many other parents, lived in fear of bombings.

Mum reached the front room with me close behind. Then she stopped. She let me run back for my dressing gown, something she wouldn't have allowed any other time. She stared at the smouldering fire in the grate, as if she should do something about it, but had forgotten what. 'I can't take any more', she said, a low murmur, not for my ears. Throwing the door open revealed a world of smoke. Mum hesitated in the doorway.

A searchlight caught a Zepp drifting above, sleek and shiny in the inky night sky.

Next door, Mr Penshurst, the butcher loudly hurried his family out of their front door. 'It's too late for the shelter, Missus.' He called to Mum, tugging on his small son's arm. The child stood staring up at the sky.

Mum didn't move forward. I wriggled to see past her.

'You'd better come to our place, Missus. This way!' He pointed to a path beside the house that led to steps with a rusty iron railing. 'We've got a cellar. It's better than nothin'. Hurry Missus. Bring y'boy.'

I didn't know the neighbours had a cellar where they hid from the bombs. I thought cellars were small rooms for vegetables, salted meat and bottled fruit. The butcher had a big family. How would we all fit? Mum didn't move. Maybe she wasn't sure about their cellar either. Then she jerked forward, grabbed my hand and followed.

'The Huns won't be happy till they've flattened every bloomin building,' Mr Penshurst said, as he ushered us into the cellar. The room wasn't as small as I thought. It had rough wooden benches, just wide enough to sit on. There were high shelves with boxes and grey blankets. There was even a faded painting of the seaside at Brighton hung crookedly on the cement wall. There was a soot-blackened lantern, a pile of newspapers and some colouring pencils along with paper, ink and stamps in a wooden orange crate. The room smelled of damp wool and kerosene. I gagged.

As he shut the door I panicked at the sudden darkness, gripping my mother's hand. A hissing match dispelled the thick blackness as the man lit a candle and set it on a small table. His wife cradled a whimpering baby and chided the small boy who'd been staring at the sky. Billy Penshurst came and sat beside me. We were in the same class at school. He took out a bag of marbles. I was itching to see them. I wondered if he had a tiger's eye. He put the bag back in his pocket and sat very still. I thought he must be very brave until saw the look in his eyes.

The candle looked like an old tree trunk, with slow yellow vines snaking down. The hot wax pooled on the table, wet and sluggish, turning white at the edges. Our candles at home sat in clear glass lanterns with shiny brass bases.

'Where's y'girl, Missus?' Mr Penshurst leant towards Mum. His voice was loud and strange in the small room. She didn't answer so I tugged on her sleeve.

'School.' Mum pulled me closer.

'Your husband is overseas? In the infantry?' The butcher persisted.

'Killed,' Mum said. 'Canada.'

'Canada?' The man's face was strange in the shadow of the blinking candle. His eyebrows crawled up his forehead. His face was flushed and the hair on his ears seemed on fire.

'Are the bloody Huns bombing the hell out of Canada too?' Billy asked, earning a jab in the ribs from an older sister.

Mum let out a long slow sigh, like the air on my bike when I had a puncture. 'He ... left years ago. Went to find gold. Joined his brother in Canada. Then enlisted. Killed on the continent somewhere.'

The butcher shook his head. His neck wobbled like white pudding.

'There'll never be an end to it,' Mum said, 'never.'

I had to lean closer to Mum to catch the words. I tapped her arm. What was wrong with her? She never talked about our father, even to us. And she wasn't even talking properly even though she was using her official voice, the one she used when she was teaching the new girls how to sew in our back sunroom so they could go the workroom in Knightsbridge and make clothes for the Red Cross.

'It's my bit for the war effort,' Mum had said, when I'd

intruded into the sunroom begging for biscuits and milk for tea. 'Off you go, Harry.' The machines made a dreadful din. I had to yell to be heard. I hated that there were giggling girls coming and going with their perfume and cigarettes, dropping wet umbrellas in the hall. Clarissa pinched me and said 'Mum's getting paid milk money for teaching them and if you didn't want to have dry porridge you'd better lay off grizzling'. Clarissa was ten years older than me and she hated sewing. Mum had been at her for years about it and she wouldn't touch the machine. But Mum said if she didn't persevere and learn, she'd be sent to the munitions factory as soon as she finished school and God-only-knows how awful that would be. It sounded like a marvellous adventure and I immediately begged to be taken there one day. Clarissa slapped the back of my head and told me not to be a complete idiot. Mum had gone really still. 'You don't know what you're talking about Harry.'

Mum's hand squeezed mine so tight I tried to pull away but she didn't notice. She stared hard at the butcher. Then out of the blue she started to ramble, 'It's not safe anywhere anymore. Our children—what are we to do with our children? Some people are sending them to the country to be safe, Mr Penshurst. I don't have family in the country. How do we keep our children safe, do you think?'

'Can't,' said the man. 'Not possible. Can't leave the little blighters underground all the time.' He laughed, a rumbling sound that filled the room. 'We've just got to get on with life missus. There's no safe place, anywhere. Not in this part o' the world.' He paused, taking the sleeping baby from his wife's arms, holding it the way he cradled a Christmas ham in the butcher shop. 'Not unless you get on a ship to the North Pole.' He snorted. 'Or Australia.'

'Australia,' Mum said, her voice rising. 'Do you think we could, Mr Penshurst? Get on a ship to Australia?'

The man's mouth fell open. He rubbed a large square hand over his forehead. 'Incredible,' he said finally, shaking his head and chins.

'Incredible,' I repeated, savouring the new word.

That was a new word for me.

The next day, Mum was a volunteer at the train station, pinning names on children going to the country to escape the bombings, away from the city, and family. When she came home, she asked for a cup of tea and said, 'I can't take any more.'

Three months later we left for Sydney.

I said my new word to everyone I met on the ship. 'We're going to Australia. Isn't that incredible!'

When we docked Mum waved a lace handkerchief frantically so her friend Miriam could see us.

'I knew her in my salad days,' Mum said.

The lost stories of Lucy Meredith Carter.

Mistakes

Bridget's **second** mistake had been to criticise Chris Green's esteemed novel *The Fault in Our Stars*. It went down about as well as Darwin's first airing of *The Origin of the Species*. It wasn't as if it had even been in English class, it was History with the much-pitied Mr Neville Mangret, their gay teacher with no dress sense who was loved as much as he was pitied.

'It's a sanitised romanticising of death and teenage love where the adults in the book are all insipid characters that play off and pander to the ill-fated teens who, ALTHOUGH DYING, (she shouted this bit), fly alone to Amsterdam, stay in a 5 star hotel where they...' At this point Bridget registered the shocked face of Mr Mangret and her gaping classmates.

Bridget stalled, frozen in embarrassment.

She never spoke in class, and even to her classmates out of class. The less they knew of her, and she of them, the better.

Bridget's **first** mistake had been to head off to school on a day when her father had been roaring drunk on his 3am journey to the toilet the night before, and had thrown her 8-week-old kitten across the room, ending its life in a hideous shattering of limbs and fur.

Bridget had raged on the toilet door until her knuckles bled but Da had swiftly shoved her aside with such rage and speed that she had fallen, reaching and grasping the kitten's mute body as she fell.

After a fart and a thorough crotch scratching, Da had shuffled off to his room muttering, immune to Bridget's screams and cursing him as 'a monster, a hideous shell of a man, a horror show of a human being'. It was the first time she'd let loose the words that caused her head to throb with hatred at the kitchen sink when he complained about the food, her slowness in cleaning up, her general stupidity.

All the while, and every time he spat those words, a voice thundered and roared inside her head, that he was wrong, this man who never saw her distinction with her schoolwork, never spoke to a single teacher of her achievements and never laid eyes on a single stroke of art she'd produced at school. Those things were locked at the school or in her mind as she chanted through house chores, 'I am more, I will be more'.

Bridget tended the body of the kitten, cotton-woolled in a shoe box. Her angry steps crunched on the icy path that had once been the route to her mother's tomato patch. There she buried her pet. Inside the house she paced with a rage she'd never experienced before. Picking up a large kitchen knife she padded into her father's room where his sterterous snoring seemed as defiant and belligerent as his daytime ravings.

Even in sleep his fists were clenched, skin pale and wrinkled. A slant of moonlight on his faced showed a pointed chin, weak jaw, even whiskers. Fine red veins flushed his cheeks and thin crooked nose.

She held the knife at his throat, just below his hairy ear, between the sinews of his throat. Calm settled through her body.

How close she had been to ending her torment. How near demise he came, the monster who used his belt and his fists on her thin body.

Da had shuddered, snorted, sat up. He stared, not seeing, not knowing, then fell back, turned onto his stomach and resumed snoring.

His eyes, so devoid of anything human were more terrifying in the semi-gloom than his bloodshot daytime tirades.

Bridget had grabbed for the knife as it slipped. It cut her palm with a satisfying pain that brought her back to reality. She padded to her room where she sat staring at the frosted windowpane until the dawning sun softened the ice, sending it downwards in faint jerking rivulets, leaving a clear view of the eucalypt scrubland.

In the morning, even without sleep, school had seemed a better option than a day in the house.

How wrong she'd been, she thought as she escaped red-faced into the maze of school hallways.

Mr Mangret hurried down the corridor after her, his

moccasins a dull, sliding thud thud on the Lino. However, before his quick steps reached Bridget, she was intercepted by the temporary Welfare Teacher, bloody old-fashioned Mrs Kennedy whose fulsome bosom kept her perpetually leaning forward when she walked, pigeon-toed in hard heeled shoes.

'I heard all that kerfuffle, Miss Galloway,' said Mrs Kennedy, gesturing towards the counselling room.

Ushered into the tiny, book-lined office, Bridget held her backpack like a shield and sank into a chair while Mrs Kennedy clattered the blinds shut, slapped her hands back and forth on the sill as if to remove a decade's dust. The room smelled stale, in that unused way, perhaps because the coat rack was overflowing with teacher's coats, left to dry or perhaps forgotten by teachers seeking a hasty escape as she did then.

'Well, now. Well, now.' Mrs Kennedy lowered herself into the chair behind the desk, unlike the regular counsellor who favoured almost knee to knee contact and penetrating gazes.

Bridget stared at the dull carpet, her usual ploy to deflect attention and expedite matters. Anyway, today she didn't care about class rules, superior teachers or punishments.

'Now, I know that I'm casual here and don't know you as well as the other teachers, dear.'

Bridget coughed. Hardly any of the teachers acknowledged her existence. Apart from Mr Mangret, the Saint of Lost Causes. She could see him pacing through the gap in the door.

Mrs Kennedy smoothed her high bun and continued, 'I

know it's very popular, and rebellious for you young people to have this whole freedom of speech thing, but your behaviour in class was unacceptable. This interrupting loudly, then storming out of class. You caused quite a stir, an uproar certainly. Oh, the students applauded, sure! But honestly?'

Bridget raised her eyes briefly, round with shock. Applause! Oh no!

'Insurgence really, anarchy, whistling, standing on desks, feet stomping—terrible!'

Bridget gasped. Had all that happened? It was hard to understand the woman. She spoke like someone's great-grandmother or a character from a television show set a few decades ago. And she rattled the words out so quickly. Bridget let the words wash over her. She pretended she was lying under one of the upturned boats on the pebbly shore at Noarlunga, the boat where the breeze still crept underneath or through a crack that allowed enough sunlight to read without the world knowing where she was.

'Have you cut your hand, child?'

'Huh.' Bridget jumped. 'Er.' Blood was seeping onto her uniform. A hastily applied Elastoplast had failed. Either that or the wound had reopened. 'Shit,' she said, snatching a handful of tissues and gripping them tightly.

'Are you alright, m'dear?' Mrs Kennedy attempted to stand but was foiled in this by her girth and the desk.

Bridget's head swirled. Hot tears gathered in her eyes but she held them back with the same tenacity that she guarded her words. Lips pursed, she sat in silence. At least her thoughts were her own. No, I'm not alright. My father murdered my kitten, my only true friend on earth and I stood over him for a full half-hour with a knife millimetres from his carotid artery but I chickened out and I wish I hadn't.

Finally she spoke. 'Yes, Mrs Kennedy, but I'd better see the nurse.' She leapt to her feet, scraped the chair backwards and ran out the door, fully aware that fulsome counsellor had no chance of successful pursuit.

Shadow Girl

The Procedure

Mike was not a hypochondriac. He was not overreacting. He wanted to clear that up from the outset, even though he had been moaning and pacing for hours. He was merely concerned with his health.

'They're only going to put a camera up your bum, Mike. Not a Mac truck,' said Jen.

Mike went stiff with disbelief. 'I am not going to dignify that with a response, Jennifer.'

Jen sighed. How had two minutes of reassurance turned into four hours of monologue that gave all the appearance of increasing Mike's angst rather than reducing it?

'At least I'm not filling up on iced chocolates with whipped cream,' he said, 'like SOME people I could mention.'

The two children had left after the first five minutes. Jenny sighed and wondered what would have happened if she'd done the same. Maybe if she kept quiet and nodded benignly...

'You're not paying attention are you?' said Mike. 'I'm

going for a walk.' Grabbing his coat Mike headed for the French doors that led to the beach track.

'Although maybe a Mac truck would...'

'Did you say what I thought you did?'

'Probably,' said Jen, wishing she had her mother's knack for diplomacy. Or that of Mike's ex-wife, who had somehow gone from frigid shrew to saint in the past year.

Jen rubbed her pregnant belly and contemplated what Freud would have to say on the matter. 'I hope you're not going to be a worrywart,' she said to her unborn son. He kicked. 'That'd be right,' she muttered.

By morning Mike's booming voice and bravado had evaporated. He alternated frantic pacing with anxious mumbling. Jen reverted to mother hen, reassuring and soothing.

A petite young Sister took his details. 'So, this is a routine colonoscopy, Mr Clements, because of family history. You have no current symptoms, correct?'

'Yes,' said Mike.

Jen's eyebrows flew up. The same statement from her mouth had started last night's lecture.

They wheeled him in. They wheeled him out. He cried with relief. He cried with joy. He began a long, convoluted conversation with the bug-eyed patient in the bed next to him. He thanked the staff, mistaking the man with the mop for a doctor. He thanked everyone who came into the room.

He thanked God. He was a man with a last reprieve in life.

He was, in fact, as high as a kite.

The Sister who came to assess him found him wiping down the bedside table with the bloodied dressing that had covered the IV site on his wrist, while Jen watched in fascination.

'I'm just cleaning up a bit,' said Mike, beaming like a cherub as he smeared blood over the surface.

The Sister looked from the red-smeared cabinet to Jen and frowned. 'I'll have that, thank you Mr Clements.'

But Mr Clements hadn't finished. Giving the Sister a demented grin he gripped the dressing and kept wiping.

'Ahhhh... okay, you can go home in twenty minutes,' said the Sister, stepping back. 'Your two hours post-procedure will be up then.'

'Two hours! Two hours? Seemed like five minutes, didn't it Jen?'

Jen, who had been sitting in a hospital chair for those hours, groaned.

A new nurse came and declared Mike fit to leave.

'Oh my God, Jen! What am I going to wear? I can't wear this gown home?'

'Your clothes are here, Mike, remember? You didn't come here naked.'

'Oh.'

The nurse buried her head in the chart. 'You just need to check at the front desk on your way out,' she said, schooling her face.

Jen threw Mike's clothes on and headed down the

corridor. 'I thought I'd have to wear the hospital gown home,' said Mike to a man clearly being admitted to the ward.

The man dropped his suitcase.

'You'll be right,' said Mike. 'S'only routine. S'lovely place.'

The man backed into a wall.

Jen yanked on Mike's arm. No small task for a heavily pregnant woman against a six foot male who had once been an athlete.

At the front desk Jen thrust the paperwork towards the receptionist, while keeping a tight grip on Mike.

Mike grabbed the papers. He brought them up to his face, then held them at arm's length. 'Is this English, Jen? He leaned closer to the receptionist.

'You can't leave without paying the theatre fee,' said the woman, unfazed by Mike. Clearly made of sterner stuff than most.

'We're in a private fund. I've already ... Mike! Leave my purse alone.' Jenny yanked unsuccessfully at her purse.

'We can't go home, Jen. Pay the nice lady.' Mike fumbled through Jen's purse.

Jen was appalled, in no small part because her husband quibbled over every expenditure, mandated the size of grocery items and checked their bank balance daily.

Jen wrenched back the purse, but Mike still had the strap. Jen turned to the receptionist. 'I had this discussion when we arrived. There is no theatre fee payable for private fund, day patients.'

'I know my job, Madam.'

'And I know that I came in early...' Jen swore quietly. An enthusiastic tug of war over her purse was increasing her ire, '... and spoke with the finance department, all to the purpose of avoiding this exact scenario.'

Mike had once more gained control of the purse and was opening it again. 'Mike! Leave that...' Jen turned to the woman. 'Why don't you get a supervisor?'

'It's after hours. The administration staff have gone for the day.' Her lips were a thin uncompromising line.

'Well,' said Jen, tired of managing a six-foot toddler and a beaurocrat, 'are the security staff still here? Do you intend to handcuff us to the chairs in the waiting room? "Can't go home" what rot!' She pointed to the relevant section on the papers.

With one brisk twist, Jen snatched the purse and shoved Mike out the door.

Mike stopped to usher an elderly woman inside with a grand gesture. 'I thought I'd have to go home in the hospital gown,' he informed her. The woman blanched.

'He was worried about getting a breeze up his skirt,' said Jen, pushing Mike towards the car.

After a brief but heroic tussle over the car keys, Jen drove home. She sunk into the lounge and was pleased to find the teenagers had eaten and retreated to their rooms.

She waited for the inevitable exhaustion to hit Mike. It missed. It hit Jen instead. Mike spent the next two hours lecturing her on manners to strangers.

In the morning he didn't remember a thing.

Almost gone...

Leah Bond, ingénue genius fashion designer fresh out of an award-winning stint at Sydney TAFE, with her own fashion line, stood in the centre of the white high-gloss kitchen of the upmarket home she shared (infrequently lately) with her much older husband, James Antoine, mystery man, entrepreneur and importer of expensive handbags. A man who spent more time in Thailand and their inner-city Sydney apartment. James Antoine employed several bodyguards that a reasonable person would be forgiven for mistaking as ex-cons. Even smart suits, supplied by James, did little to downplay this impression.

James Antoine had lately expressed serious concerns for his wife's mental health to anyone of their acquaintance, anyone who would listen to his narrative of Leah's apparent unravelling.

Leah was currently undertaking a strange occupation that would have added credence to her husband's claims, that is, if they hadn't known the real story, which is often not what anyone thinks it is. Leah crushed several flowers in her hands, rending and tearing them. Destroying their annoying, bloody cheerful little daisy faces. It felt good to be doing something, however small and impotent.

She placed their remains on the black marble bench and began to dice them, smaller and smaller, mesmerised by the rocking motion of the knife and the sharp metallic sounds of blade on stone. Her hands were green-stained and slimy, but still she pared, this way, that way, as if she were preparing basil for pesto. Something ordinary.

Life had been ordinary once.

Leah stared at her reflection in the stainless steel range-hood. Fear haunted her eyes. Mascara had blended with her tears and made a grotesque path down her cheeks. A purple bruise was beginning to show on her neck. Her face belonged in a horror movie. Was she losing her mind? James seemed to think so.

She wiped her face with a linen tea towel. James hated that, she'd have to throw it out. She stared at it—smeared with black and green, indelible stains.

Her hands began to shake uncontrollably. She slid to the floor beside the huge metal bucket containing the rest of the daisies. She'd only destroyed a few, there were still dozens. Romance, she decided, began and ended with flowers. The profuse arrangements of courtship, then the showy garlands of apology. And of course, the guilt bouquet, the most extravagant of all. Life with James had jerked through many phases of excess, always excess.

Leah caressed a daisy, turning its face toward her. 'It's not your fault,' she said, 'you're only flowers.'

The phone rang. She jumped. She'd better answer it. It could be James, asking if she'd received the flowers. If she didn't get there in time there'd be more hell to pay.

'Hello,' she said, flinching at the rasp in her voice.

'Are you all right Leah? You haven't done anything stupid have you?' James' voice had an icy edge.

'I'm fine, honey. Just a tickle in my throat, dust, cleaning.'

'Are you sure? You haven't been yabbering on the phone to one of your friends have you? Stephanie says there's still a mountain of work to be done for the show.'

'Tell my sister,' Leah said, 'that everything is on track.' She ground her teeth. 'Stephanie worries too much.'

'She cares. She's your sister.'

Leah's hand cramped on the phone. *My sister, and your spy.* 'I'm putting you on speaker phone James. I ... have my hands full here.'

'You know I hate that Leah. Anyway, I haven't got much time. Did you get the flowers?'

'Yes. I got them.' *All six dozen of them.*

James was silent.

'They're lovely. Thanks, honey.'

'Well, I wanted ... to make it up to you.'

Leah froze. Not the apology, the contrition that looped back to recrimination, then blame.

'Leah? You there?'

'Yes.'

'I'm sorry babe, but I have to go overseas, urgent business.'

'How long?'

'Two weeks. I'm sorry to miss the show ... and everything...'

Leah tried to concentrate. Two weeks, two weeks free of James. He was cajoling now. She mustn't seem pleased.

'But James, you promised.'

'I'll make it up to you. Bring you something wonderful from Thailand. Anyway, we can skype. Every day. It will be just as if I was there with you. Just don't do anything stupid, like before ... okay honey bun?'

'I'm fine I said.'

Like before ... before when James had gashed her wrist with the quick slice of a knife, called the ambulance and babbled on about her mental state while she bled like a pig, protesting his version of facts that was rejected out of hand by the ambos and emergency staff. However, because it was the first incident she hadn't been admitted to the Mental Health Unit. That wouldn't be the case next time.

After Leah put the phone down, a tap on the glass door startled her.

It was Dyan, from next door. She pointed to the lock on the sliding door and mouthed, 'Open it, now!'

'I was just dicing...' Leah said.

'Daisies?' Dyan folded her arms. 'Don't bullshit me, Leah. I work in a women's refuge.'

'Oh.'

'Yes, *oh*! James isn't here I take it? Ah, no, of course not. You wouldn't have let me in ... and don't tell me, James doesn't even know that you and I are acquainted. I'm not on that teeny weeny list of "suitable friends". Dyan mimicked quotation marks with her hands. 'Will James, Lord and Master, be home anytime soon? I wouldn't want to rock the balance of the high-walled kingdom.' Dyan raised an eyebrow, her face stony, as if she would relish doing precisely that.

Leah stood silently in the centre of the kitchen.

Dyan leaned on the bench, eyes narrowed.

Leah gripped her hand and flinched in pain. 'Dyan... Fuck!'

'Show me.'

Leah lifted her arm and unwound the bandage. 'It's my wrist. Months old now, but I get...'

'Keloid, yes, I see. Let me dress it. You need the right cream for it.'

Leah paled. 'I know. I just...'

'Haven't gotten around to it. I do understand sweetie, more than you know. Things that are hidden always come into the light. What happened? Was it James? Can't have been you, you're useless with your left hand.'

Tears streamed down Leah's face. 'The ambos didn't believe me. James had them thinking I was off my rocker.'

'There's a word for that.'

'I know Dyan. Gaslighting.'

'Have you had enough, Leah?'

'What?'

'You know what I mean.'

Leah nodded.

Dyan sighed, then, when she spoke, there was a new gravity to her words as her eyes pinned Leah. 'I thought I'd let you know that Peter and I will be moving his mother into the granny flat at the back of our place. It will be a bit noisy and busy over at ours for a few days. Workmen, **removalists...**'

'Removalists?'

'Yes ... they're usually thrilled with a return load, the truck will be here first thing in the morning.' Dyan brushed Leah's hair behind an ear.

Leah met her gaze. 'In the morning...?'

'...first thing.'

*Shadow Girl

Billy and me

I was named Kate, after my mother's favourite sister. They were the youngest of eight, separated from the others by illness and immaturity. Mum had Bright's Disease and was wrapped in blankets to sweat the fever out. She got over it. Aunt Kate had asthma and never got over it. Mum had me and Aunt Kate had Billy. We were so much alike we said we should've been twins. I had an older brother and Billy had a younger sister. Neither of them got us at all. We were both curious and chatted away like crickets, roaming around our back yards looking for treasure and creatures. My brother said we were like a toothache. We didn't care. We were five.

Our families didn't hug much. Billy and me ran round together, one arm around the other most of the time, giggling and looking. We hugged the world. Mum was never sick. Except when she had all her teeth out. Her mouth dribbled blood and nonsense when she came home from the hospital. Dad said the anaesthetic made her silly. It still worried me because she was never silly so I sat by her bed. She kept trying to get up, all wobbly and loose. I just stayed and put her legs back in the bed. Dad said I didn't have to do that, but I couldn't stop. Billy's mother was in and out of hospital, drowning for want of air to breathe. We were ten.

Mum became a shop manager and Aunt Kate took in sewing, piece work for a factory. Mum unloaded delivery trucks beside the men. The men struggled to work as hard as she did. Some didn't like her much. She said it was because of petticoat government. Aunt Kate ran out of breath in the winter and died on the way to hospital. The next year Billy's father died and he came to live with us. One morning I got up and he was gone. His room was empty, not even a hint of him. It was as if I'd dreamed him. Mum tried to push on my leg in church so I'd kneel down with the congregation to pray. I slapped her hand away and told her she could have God all to herself. I was fifteen.

*The Northerly

Before

I remember sitting on the rim of the universe, dangling my legs. Waiting. For that gentle angel-shove off the bench at the door to heaven.

The boy sitting beside me looks a little worried. 'Do you think we'll be angels or devils on earth?'

'Oh!' I say. (It's a question I hadn't considered).

'Both, I guess,' I say, shrugging.

'Will there be Maths I wonder,' he muses.

I shudder.

The others on the bench are squirming now. Their minds are winding back, ticking like miniature metronomes, back to the almost-zero state of mind necessary to be born on earth.

'Stop shoving,' one says.

I exchange a look with the boy. He shakes his head. 'That doesn't bode well,' he says.

The angel comes; the one that pushes us off into the cosmos.

'Why do we have to be pushed?' asks the boy.

'It prepares you for life on earth,' says the angel, standing in front to deliver a last few words to each of us.

'Lily.' The angel uses my earth name, as her wings flutter to her sides, and remain still as midnight.

'Yes. Do I get some other names?'

'You ask too many questions,' says the boy.

I give him the "who's being a hypocrite look now" look.

'You might,' says the angel, 'it's up to the parents you're born to.'

'They seem nice,' I say, peering down. 'Are they?'

The angel stretches out a wing so I can't see the parents. That doesn't perturb me.

'They might be a bit older, but they've never given up on each other. They're not the type to give up on a kid … child,' I say, pushing my luck. We're not supposed to ask for reassurances. It's a trust thing.

The angel sighs. 'They'll probably give you another name, the name of someone who's really special to them.'

'So Pocohontas is out then.' I mutter, wondering why no one else is asking questions.

'They'll like me,' I say, to no one in particular. 'They've waited ages for a girl. Especially the mother person.'

'You won't be exactly what she expects.'

The angel's wings begin a fluttering tremor that creates a loud breeze.

When the angel speaks again, I struggle to hear. 'Is anyone up for…?'

In my ignorant bliss, I say, 'sure, I will!'

The next thing I know, we're falling, although it's more like a drift. I turn to the boy, 'Did the angel ask if anyone was up for three lifetimes in one?'

But the boy is sucking his thumb, his mind has slipped to where it should be.

'Bother,' I say, wondering why it's taking so long for my baby brain to kick in.

The funeral crashers

Ephram and Harry were involved in a class war. Ephram was the newcomer. Harry felt justified in thinking that Ephram owed him a certain respect. Even if it was just for seniority. The others joked about Harry's posh accent, but bore him no ill will for it. After all, some of them had come from highflying backgrounds. Anyway, Harry was a fixture, one who could be relied on, no matter what—and that counted for a lot in Cardboard City where life was pared back to the essentials.

Harry not only had a bigger cardboard box to climb into at night, it was also a Jaguar car parts box. Nothing could top that. Certainly not Bill's GE refrigerator cardboard box.

Harry complained when Ephram thrashed in his sleep, and that started Ephram making remarks about Harry's wheezing snore.

'A chip on your shoulder is what you have, Thunder Cloud,' said Harry.

'Why do you call me that? Is there no pride left for a

man?' Ephram shoved his icy fingers into his pockets.

'That's where you're wrong. A man's dignity isn't something to throw away—that's what you've done—tossed it aside. No one took it from you.'

'You wouldn't understand.'

Harry shrugged.

'I guess it depends on how far you fell to get here,' muttered Ephram, unfolding his army surplus sleeping bag. It was the only thing he had taken from home. Cindy wouldn't notice it was missing. He didn't dare take anything else. He would have loved photos of the children, but entering the house would have been inviting trouble. Their alarm system would have spelled his doom. Her alarm system now.

'You act as if you're the only one in the world to hit rock bottom,' said Harry. 'We all have our story.'

'What's yours?' asked Ephram, his interest piqued.

'You're not ready to hear it,' said Harry, turning to arrange his bedding.

The others ignored them. It wasn't a place where confidences were readily shared. Anonymity brought a level playing field. Shared reminiscences over the carefully tended fires were sparse. The past was behind. There was always someone who raked on the others' nerves, but they soon learned it didn't pay. What did it matter in the scheme of things? When one was homeless the next meal and the anticipation of some treasure that might be found in the dumpsters at the rear of the row of shops near the railway were far more pressing concerns.

Harry stayed later than usual by the fire that night. His cough had worsened. For once, Ephram was silent.

Rising early, Ephram rolled up his bedding and tipped his cap at Old Benjamin, who returned the gesture with a nod. By tacit agreement, Old Benjamin watched over their possessions during the day while they walked the streets, busked, begged or simply scrounged. For this service he was rewarded with small portions of food at night, which he hungrily devoured. No one asked any questions—not here. It was whispered that Young Jason had a job. Sergeant Joe, a man with military-like habits had seen him washing up in the subway toilets. Jason returned every night, often with an extra portion for Old Benjamin.

Ephram wandered aimlessly through the light snowflakes of the New York winter, when the wind brought snow in blizzard sheets. Looking across the road he saw a local church with the doors wide open. No one would notice him. He slipped into a far corner of the back seat. Head down, he rubbed his hands vigorously.

'You here for the funeral?' It was the cultured voice of Harry.

'Oh, no. There's a funeral?' said Ephram, his antipathy for Harry lost in embarrassment.

Harry laughed a low rumble. 'What did you think that was at the front? A large timber flower holder?'

Ephram raised pained eyes. 'We'll have to leave.'

'Why, it's a small affair. There are only a few rows right down the front filled.'

Ephram raised himself slightly out of the pew, but sat

back down when the heavy wooden doors closed. The two men sat in silence. The music began. It was unexpectedly joyful—at variance with the sombre surroundings. The words filtered down. Apparently the deceased had been a trombone player.

'We'd better leave now th...' Ephram's words were cut off by an older woman in an extraordinary black hat with a vibrant fuschia flower.

'Come on gentlemen, the wake is through here,' she said. Her voice sounded brash, but her smile, and gloved hand on Harry's arm, spoke otherwise.

Harry beamed.

Ephram blushed. 'We couldn't possibly...'

'...refuse,' said Harry, rising and tucking the woman's hand through the crook of his arm. Ephram followed, his face etched with tension.

'Can you believe that?' said Ephram.

The two men stood by the fire that Old Benjamin had tended. His toothless smile showed pleasure at the delights the men had brought him. 'Were y'at a weddin'? One of them gala dos?' he asked, then scurried back to his corner.

'I think this is the first time I've seen you smile, Ephram,' said Harry.

'Might do it again if you stop calling me Thunder Cloud.'

'Ha.'

'What a spread, hey?'

'What a woman,' said Harry, producing a small, scented piece of paper with a phone number.

'You old son of a gun ... surely you don't mean to...'

'Why not? I'm as good as any man. Not everyone is judged by their wealth, Thun ... ah ... Ephram.'

'I've got news for you. It's a material world, old man.'

'You'd be surprised.'

'You're 100% right about that, Harry. Surprised would be an understatement.'

Harry gazed through narrowed eyes but said nothing.

'Truce?' Ephram extended his hand.

Harry shook it with a wry smile.

As Ephram tumbled into his first dreamless sleep since the train accident, he saw Harry staring at the slip of paper the woman had given him.

Underbelly comes to the suburbs

(not entirely fiction!)

As with most suburbs we were all used to the occasional egging of the house and prank phone calls but one school holiday the vandals decided to 'up the ante' in my neck of the woods. My security sensor was broken.

Then the nonsense really began. It was plain to me and everyone else living near me that I was a favourite target. My letter box disappeared, then returned, then disappeared and the bricks that formed the foundation for the letterbox were strewn across my front lawn. The KEEP OUT sign from the old man's property across the street was put in the front of my place. This man was an elderly man whose wife was dying of cancer and he had ongoing problems with these teenage boys cutting through his property, distressing him. About 100 copies of the local newspaper, the Lakes Mail, that had been delivered to our area appeared in front of my house, strewn everywhere. Various items on my back patio were broken or disappeared.

I awoke the next morning to find the little old lady who

lived across the road standing barefoot and shivering with cold in her driveway. She was regarding my house with confusion and dismay. There in my front yard where my letter box should have been was an old wooden one—hers.

That necessitated me visiting her and introducing myself as a nice respectable woman who was very embarrassed to have someone else's letterbox in my front yard and was not a gangster or a thug. She was most relieved by this reassurance and soon her husband came out to join her. A conversation about the growing vandalism in the street ensued.

They were Yugoslavian and the old man apologised for not having his glasses on.

'I seena some boys agoin' acrossa my place ona bikes in the fronta my housa, but I couldna see whata they looka like because I can'ta see me owna wife iffen she isna right in fronta me face.'

At this explanation his voice went up a notch as he leaned confidingly toward me. *But they hatea you!'* he added dramatically. On gaining no response from me on the subject of my neighbourhood status of The Target he again repeated, 'They hatea you!'

He eyed me with the gaze of one who desperately desired to know what a bland blonde woman could have done to inspire such vengeance. I wasn't quite sure myself but had a nagging feeling that it had something to do with me ordering certain of my son's 'acquaintances' off my property in the past because they appeared to be smoking a substance that was illegal in some countries (this one included!).

After talking to neighbours on both sides I found that doorbells were being rung at night every half hour or so and fires had been lit in the street in front of the home of my neighbours, Diane and Barrie Ridgway.

I then discovered that my Wizz bin had also disappeared.

I rang the Police who arrived swiftly and let me know in no uncertain terms that they wished to leave in an even swifter fashion. Although they quite often displayed a fondness for informing me on past occasions that there was nothing they could do they appeared a little offended when I repeated this same claim back to them.

'I guess because they are minors you are powerless and they can just make monkeys out of you guys,' I said. 'Horrible to be impotent.' I sighed, keeping my distance... Anyway, *I thought* this was a fairly accurate translation of what they'd previously said. The eyes of the sharp-faced policeman narrowed, then jaw clenched, he listened.

I took a deep breath and went for broke. I began with the history of events that had been happening in our community at the end of our crescent—about the fires in the street, pranks with my letterbox, harassment of the dying, blind, frail and those prone to heart attacks, stolen property, ringing of doorbells, egging of houses and accidentally threw in a few things that happened last year at Halloween just because I got up a bit of speed. (I had several youths come to my house at Halloween, and when I said I had no lollies for them, one had tried to enter the house forcibly. I had throw my weight against the door to stop them coming inside.)

They left.

My Wizz bin was back in 45 minutes.

In spite of the success of this mission immediately as I left the house the next day in the car, one of the boys who had vandalised the area rang our house and gave my son a 'mouthful'. My son rang me and told me the number.

So for the first time in a long time I *DIDN'T* ring the Police. I *VISITED* the Police station on the way home and gave them the phone number my son had given me. They rang it while I was there and had a firm conversation with the boy who denied making the call and gave the policewoman quite a bit of attitude. She took this with calm but steely control and ordered him to come in the next day for questioning.

I was a bit bug eyed at the desk hearing her side of the conversation as I chatted to a burly cop at the desk. The female officer reminded the boy that he was already in trouble for theft and vandalism and they could easily check phone records to find the truth.

I told them I could do better than that and went home and literally dragged Barrie, my peaceful passive neighbour out of his garden by the shirt sleeve as he pruned his roses. I told him to hurry up and get his digital camera as my phone had Calling Number Identification with the time, date and number displayed and I needed him to take a photo to give the police.

I followed him around his house making sure he went at twice his usual speed and chatted to his wife Diane as I hassled him. She didn't seem to mind me harassing him and even joined in with a '*get moving, Barrie!*' once or twice herself. They were the ones that had fires lit in front of their house and also constant door bell ringing. Barrie came over to my place and with the meticulous style that had been his trademark as a bank manager, he took the photo, printed it and I handed it in at the Police Station.

'Bloody marvellous', said the burly, smiling officer at the desk. 'That will be really helpful in the interview tomorrow, let him dig his own grave then we'll show him this. Bloody marvellous.'

II

Not again! I couldn't believe it! Honestly what had I done in a former life??

Let me start at the beginning. I sometimes rented a room out, or two or three. As part of my poverty management plan. I had to let my financial manager go, (oh alright, I never had one). Because I had my mother with me a couple of times to convalesce I hadn't had someone renting for a while so I accepted two guys through the real estate who were working nearby and commuting interstate. I don't have a big house, but had turned the lounge room into a bedsit. They did a stretch of 12 hour shifts, showered at work and ate out. I hardly saw them.

Matthew, tenant/boarder No. 2 was a tall well-built guy in his mid-twenties with some really impressive looking tattoos, but a thoroughly gentle nature. He was easy going and relaxed, until... He arrived back from work one afternoon and sought me out while I was watering the garden.

'Do you know the phone number for the local police?' he asked, his eyes slits of steel.

I rattled it off quickly. His eyebrows rose at my speedy reply. I shrugged. He hurried off to phone the cops. After he'd done that he came to chat, which loosely translated, meant turn the air blue about 'people' who had nothing better to do than thieve from hardworking men. And they were hard working; putting in twelve hour days, for eleven days straight, before having three days off. The thieves had picked the wrong guy on the wrong day. Suffice it to say that in recent times, 'life had been a bitch'. Well there was something about an ex in there...

They had taken his GPS and about $500 worth of electronic gear he'd just bought. He had a mutter to his mates, then had a mutter to me. I told him about my episodes with 'Vandals and thieves' (see related stories) and I confided the name and location of the 'usual suspect'. I told him of the ongoing problems, electricity turned off, TV connections unplugged, bolts taken out, security lights broken, things stolen – the list seemed endless.

'Mmm,' said Matthew, 'might do a random walk around the neighbourhood, visit a few people. I'll see if anyone saw anything—and visit that kid.'

Now one doesn't offer advice to grown men renting rooms, but in the interest of the success of his mission I casually suggested he might have less trouble 'making his point' if his tattoos were clearly visible. To my surprise he went and changed into a muscle shirt. Off he went, his lithe

6 foot frame ramrod straight and determined. He was wearing his thin sunglasses. Only a single-celled amoeba would have missed his attitude. He had a casual chat with the neighbours on both sides, and across the road, and then he was out of sight. I went inside—he didn't need me staring after him, like a nervous puppy. He was back soon.

'Yeah, that kid's the one alright. Looked as guilty as sin as soon he opened the door.' Matthew went on to relate the rest of the conversation that had me gaping. Being around teenage boys and young men, I thought I'd heard everything. Apparently not.

'I told the little sh#t I'd be back in 30 minutes for my stuff and if it wasn't there I would &#*% him. I told him, 'I know people who know people' and if he wanted a peaceful life he'd leave this house alone for the rest of his miserable life.'

Oh crap, I thought. I'd been calm up to this point, but then my mind ran off to the reprisals I might suffer when these guys left. There were two men staying with a third guy arriving the next day on the same contract job. What then for me? What if I got it wrong? I would have chewed my nails, but I had none left. I said nothing, deciding to keep to myself for the designated 30 minutes. I nervously went back to watering.

I was just washing up when Matthew came back through the door. He was loaded up with all of his stolen stuff. I'm not often speechless, general anaesthetic being the only proven time, but that day my jaw was on the floor. Everything was in its original boxes and plastic bags.

'I suppose you're going to tell me you even got the

receipts,' I said, when I found my voice.

'Better than that,' he said, lifting the lid of the cardboard box back to reveal some writing.

'I got the little creep to get a pen and write down the name of his friend and accomplice.'

My eyes were like saucers and his friend, the other boarder Deakin, came to the scene equally stunned. There on the box lid, was not only a name, but an address and phone number. 'I don't think the cops get this kind of result,' I mumbled.

'Still got to 'visit' the other prick,' said Matthew.

'Oh,' was all I could manage. I wasn't privy to the details of the other visit—and quite frankly just wanted to lie down. A man's world belonged to a man, not a wuss like me.

Matthew and Deakin's friend, Danno arrived the next day. He had a huge double cabin Ute with logos and bull bars and other stuff—forgive me for the lack of information—I'm a female. This guy was older and tougher, and sported even more impressive 'tatts'.

The guys had a barbeque at the back, sat me down with a beer and recounted the story. With my head already swimming, I was glad for the beer. Matthew and Danno went for a drive. Danno's arrival couldn't have been timed better. After Matthew's subtle statement that 'he knew people who knew people' it must have looked like the 'big boss from out of town' had arrived.

Matthew and Danno arrived back to say they'd visited the culprits again because the security codes for Matthew's gear was missing. 'I think we scared the crap out of the whole family,' said Matthew.

'Certainly made the father sh#t himself,' said Danno.

The thought that, for once, someone bigger was on my side was strangely exhilarating. I tried to turn off the worry of how it could all go terribly wrong after they left, and enjoyed the moment.

I'm living in 'Underbelly', only on the right side,' I exclaimed. They all grinned.

The next day I opened the door to a strange man. He appeared to be trembling slightly. He introduced himself as the father of one of the boys. He wanted to know if I could ask Matthew to phone him and handed me his mobile number. Slightly emboldened by having 'back up' for the first time in history I announced that it 'wasn't my business', but I didn't think Matthew would want to waste valuable mobile phone time on someone who'd already ripped him off.

'Why don't you come back when they're home?' I suggested helpfully.

He appeared to put this idea on a par with being alone with a hungry crocodile and began jabbering on with other options.

'You really have to speak to Matthew,' I said. 'I'm just the landlady.' I adopted a blank look. 'Of course, these boys have been vandalising and stealing from me in the past, so personally I am going to apply for AVOs so they stay away from my property. But that's just me.'

'Get up here!' he yelled over his shoulder.

I looked down to the car and there were the two culprits. How had I missed that? They came quickly to the door.

They all apologised, gave me their mobile phone numbers and gratefully left.

If the boarders were chuffed when I referred to them as 'The Underbelly Crew', they didn't show it. I wondered how it would be when they left. To my astonishment not a single leaf on a tree was touched.

*I'm not broken, I'm just different.

My Fair Lady

The old woman shivered on the park bench, causing several of the petals of the decaying rose on her lap to fall to the ground. She was kitted out in an array of layered garments, a bright pink floral frock that had seen better days, a wide, lurid, lime-green belt, fastened over a dull grey cardigan and a pair of purple leggings. There was a sequined purse with a long chain that was wound around a slender forearm, creating a dark bruise.

The woman spoke slowly and clearly. 'I can do without anybody I choose. I have my own soul, my own spark of divine fire.' She fiddled with a tired feathered fascinator that tilted precariously on her head. She pulled the cardigan around her bony body.

'Ah, 'tis a bitter wind that it is,' she said, 'I'll be sellin' no flow'rs today, I feah.'

Strangers walking past bent to ask soft questions, but she continued to talk to herself while she delicately arranged her faded long skirts.

Hope Benton, physiotherapist and mother of three year

old Damien, approached the woman, sensing the old woman's dislocation. 'Are you alright, Madam?' she asked. Damien ran to his mother and knocked the bench.

'Nah then, Freddy: look wheah y'gowin, deah.' The old woman's voice had changed to a course Cockney accent.

'Who's that, Mummy?' asked a boyish voice.

'Eliza Doolittle,' said Hope, shocked as memories of reading George Bernard Shaw's 'Pygmalion' surfaced.

'Y'know me then, luvvy? Fancy some flow'rs, deah? Wot's y'name, pet?'

'Hope...ah Benton,' Hope sat, reached into her handbag and took out a mobile phone. '... er ... this is my son...'

The boy tilted his head to look at the old woman. 'My name isn't Freddy, it's Damien,' he said.

'Oh, never you pay me no mind, my deah. I calls everyone Freddy. S'easier y'see.'

While the old woman and the boy chatted Hope phoned the police.

The woman began to cough, a hacking, rasping sound.

Damien thumped her on the back.

'Nah, Freddy, ev'ry winter I gets the chills.'

The police arrived and the gentle nature of the old woman changed. 'Leave me be, y'feckless Bobbies. I aint doin' a liv'n soul no 'arm.'

Hope turned questioning eyes towards the police officer.

'Thanks, ma'am. She lives in a nursing home nearby and every now and then she escapes.' The officer shrugged.

The old woman glared at the officer. 'Just you wait, 'enry

'iggins, just you wait!'

'Who is she? She was talking normally then started sprouting lines from... well... My Fair Lady... you know the...'

'Yes, love. She's what we call a regular. Name's Beatrice Ormiston—an actress at one time. Only minor roles mind you, but apparently her crowning achievement was being understudy as Eliza Doolittle. I don't know why she chooses the first Act.'

'So, you've seen...'

'Yeah, well, you know the wife dragged me along...'

'Right.' Hope laughed. 'Will she be okay?'

'Sure, the nurses will sort her out...'

'I outlived him, you know.' The old woman spoke in clipped upper-class tones.

Hope's forehead creased.

'Yes, Beatrice, you won,' said the officer, shaking his head.

'Wha...' muttered Hope.

'Look, I shouldn't ... you're not a journalist are you?' asked the burly policeman. He hesitated, but the young woman had been so kind. It had been days before anyone had found Beatrice the last time.

'Do I look like a journalist?' asked Hope, holding one handle of the child's stroller and struggling to keep a large carry bag from dragging on the ground.

'Sorry. We have to be careful.'

'...I won out in the end. That I did. Philandering waster that he was...I stayed with that beastly man, never complaining, biding my time. Waiting for freedom. Waiting and waiting.'

'Who is she now? Another part in a play?'

'No, she's herself at the moment. Won't last long though. Then she'll go back to Eliza... always Eliza. She hated her husband you see, but was too proud to leave him. Was always polite to his face, but pure venom behind his back. He suffered from gas poisoning in the war and wasn't expected to live...so she waited...'

'Oh. What happened to him?'

'He struggled with his lungs, but lasted remarkably well. Only died last year. They owned a mansion, but by the time he died she'd lost her memory and didn't even know where she lived, couldn't even find her way home from the nearest street corner. Turned out, he'd been holding her together.'

'So she got dementia ... around the same time...?

'Hard to say, really. She wasn't a great actor, but she was a good one. She would ignore him, then chuckle to her friends that she was Dame Vague and say how much she was looking forward to living alone in the mansion. Whenever something was unpleasant, she acted as though she hadn't caught on... So, no-one really noticed how far she'd slipped. Of course, she couldn't hide it when she began to regress to 'Eliza'. At first everyone thought it was a joke, her husband humoured her in it. I guess the act became real.'

'So did she ever get to live alone in the mansion?'

The policeman laughed. 'Not even for day. The husband had to put her into care years before he died. Spent a fortune on a good facility for her. He wasn't well himself.

He hired a nurse and domestic staff and died at home. Well, I'd better...'

'Oh, sorry to keep you. She seemed so ... lost. What a story?'

'That's life, truth's stranger than fiction they say.'

There was a bang as the old woman slapped the police car.

'Ah-ah-ah-ow-ow-ow-oo, get orf with yer, Freddy,' she shouted, 'This 'ere taxi won't drive its flamin' self.'

8 word story

Bank emptied, she waited for her internet lover.

Anyone but him, please God!

His every breath was a rasping struggle. He sucked air into a chest that heaved and swelled like an ancient tide on a decimated beach. He was holocaust; he was dying. The only spark left was in his sunken grey eyes.

The ambulance trolley squeaked as it rolled down the corridor of Male Medical. The old man rattled. He was propped up, in semi-recumbent position. He would never lie down again. When he spoke, his voice was a strangled whisper. The ambulance men with their big square shoulders chatted to each other; effortlessly young and full of life.

It was late in the day. We settled him into cool white sheets. We unfolded a woven cotton blanket, spreading it over his thin frame. He waved it away. The weight was too much. He was accompanied by his daughter, a tall and graceful woman with measure step and quiet control. She bent low over her father, placing her ear close to his mouth to catch his words. I shrank back; I could never do that. Please no. To be so close to a man more dead than alive; more departed than present.

I bargained with God. I was spent; beaten. '*Enough*,' I pleaded. I would do anything, take care of anyone, *just not him*, anything but that. I was too vulnerable, too human. I was clinging to myself the way the old man was clinging to life. And I feared myself more than I feared his death. But I also surely feared his death; his final journey over the River Styx. How would it affect me watching him die? I had never seen a dead body. That empty building left after the essence of humanity has departed.

God ignored me. When I left the ward that evening at the end of my shift I checked the allocation sheet for the next morning. There was his name at the top of my patient list. I railed at God, the universe and life itself. I had been given more than I could bear. I woke stiff with fear; weighed down with dread. I shuffled onto the ward with leaden rebellious feet. My heart was heavy; he was so soon to die. I would attend to him first, get this burden out of the way; over with.

He was propped up exactly as he had been the night before. Alive; still. His eyes turned slowly towards me. There was no fear in them to match mine; only calm acceptance. And intelligence, this surprised me. I thought his mind must surely have betrayed him in the same way his body had; but no. I bent to hear his words.

I leaned in close to hear death's whisper. He was in

the waiting room for heaven or hell, and I was trapped there with him. The vibration of his voice felt strange against my ear; so little breath, so little life. He was a shipwreck that refused to sink and leave us surviving mortals to believe in 'beauty' and 'forever'. He was a monument to the futility in us all.

The other nurses seemed far away with their laughing strides down the corridors. The murmur of daily complaint and the metallic sounds of a nurses' world barely reached me. Outside there was bundling of linen, ringing of phones, buzzing of call bells. A doctor's low rumble as he gave instructions, wheels on trolleys, aromas from the kitchen—these intruded; only a little, then receded.

I ministered to him. His name was Jack. I asked if he wanted a shower or a bed bath. I posed my questions so that a simple nod would suffice. His lips strained at the side—a smile? There was no whimpering despondency in his manner. No hasty frustration in the wave of his hands. I took my time. When he was shaved, cleaned and dressed in new flannelette pyjamas a skeletal hand beckoned me to his ear. A tear was glistening in his eye.

"Thank you," he whispered, "you're beautiful."

I loved him. I hadn't wanted to be near him; now I didn't want to leave. I read to him. I told him about the world outside his door. I nursed him for five days. Five privileged beautiful days and when he died he took the inevitable piece of me with him, but he left the bountiful gift of the beauty of his spirit.

When I next recognised fear in my heart, I would not shrink but accept; embrace. Forevermore I could sit with death, and not tremble. God had taken me to the edge, then freed me.

He had not granted my request, but had gifted me with something more—something immeasurably precious.

We took him to the basement morgue, Sam, Estelle and I. Sam was a senior nurse; a tall blonde Canadian with a gentle nature. Estelle and I were new and had never been to the morgue. We were skittish and afraid. Sam smiled indulgently at us. All the way down to the morgue in the lift, Estelle and I talked too much; nervous chatter, filling the silence.

Sam understood. We told him that we were glad it was him with us on our first time and not one of the 'mug lair' male nurses who took every opportunity to torment new nurses with practical jokes. He grinned broadly and reassured us, telling us exactly what it was like, what we would see and experience.

We positioned Jack's body and I patted the sheet with an affectionate farewell.

The water pipes in the old building rattled loudly; an exact replica of Jack's breathing. Estelle and I let out identical screams and clung to Sam.

"Well," he said. "This is better than anything a practical joke gets; two women in my arms screaming."

Our screams became hesitant giggles of relief. We walked from the cold room, down the cool corridor; into the warm sunlight; arm in arm. We crossed the gardens jumping plants and walking on the forbidden grass - defying the rules. We were young; we were alive.

As I looked up, enjoying the warmth of the sun on my face, I remembered my last conversation with Jack.

"God sent you to me," he whispered.

"No Jack, God *sent you to me.*"

*Signs Publishing

Ancient grief

Nonfiction

Her eyes are shiny-bright with unshed tears. Like hardened diamonds, unseeing but not unknowing. What she now knows she cannot share, cannot face. She sits amidst the others in the low care ward, in the place for which she has no name.

She is 89, and for all those around her she is essentially alone, surrounded by people; but isolated by grief. Whether bending over the dining table or clutching her walking stick with grim determination she still manages to appear erect, although she has not been straight-of-back for many years.

Her son died a week ago. He was 71—in the eyes of many, an old man, but not to her, she who is older than him by the years of her motherhood. She measures all the years and days by her sons, now two. She rose early the day after he died, putting two curlers in her hair as she usually did. Then took them out again before going to the dining room for breakfast. As she always did. She puts her make-up on as usual, but now with trembling hand, heavier and imprecise. She walks a little slower. Stays a little longer at the table. She brushes the crumbs from her skirt with an absent gaze that glances, but never connects with her fellow residents. These little signs are the only indication of her breaking heart.

We do not know how to go to her, in this world of her devastation. She is from a generation where emotions have 'their place'. She will not allow us entrance to her grief, so we must leave her there, in the memorial of her own choosing.

Reaching out with guarded hand, she gently touches her son's face in the photograph by her bedside, when she thinks we're not watching. The tears struggle down her wrinkled cheeks. She hears a door open. She is so afraid to be seen exposed and vulnerable that she flees to the bathroom, to the shower, and the comfort of solitary grieving.

These are the routines she clings to desperately every day for two weeks. But like an autumn leaf she falls. Unable to fall into her grief, she falls in the shower. We find her naked and bleeding, broken and alone. The ambulance comes and she is stoic still.

When she returns from the hospital she is a little more stooped, a little more fragile. Then she begins to sit in the foyer where she has never sat before. When we ask her why, she focuses us with clear, direct eyes. 'I am waiting for the school bus.'

Leaving our reality, she has found her own. She has wandered to a safe place; a place still inhabited by everyone precious to her. Grieving and memories have combined in this new world. She lets us lead her. She doesn't ask to return to her room as once was her custom. 'Take me home,' she whispers.

*Mater Misericordiae Grieve Writing Award.

Ancient Love

Gwen is gentle of spirit and fiercely loving. She touches his face as she asks each question. His hungry eyes follow her every move. It is the day of the Christmas Party at the nursing home.

As the ward RN, I am a bystander in so many ways to this ancient love. This meshing and joining of two souls. This joyous reunion, this daily miracle. They are old, these two; old and frail. He sits in his chair, propped up by the pillow I made him in an attempt to do something for him, to rid me of the desperate sense of helplessness I feel towards them both.

His mouth is momentarily soft, not presently twisted from the stroke he suffered twelve years ago. He is relaxed as he sits in the billowy chair that cushions his ancient bones.

He is quiet now, rapt in the music of the Christmas carollers as they warble energetically. He is no longer articulate of speech. The phrases he speaks are basic and simple since the stroke claimed so many of his faculties but not his indomitable spirit.

In some indefinable way he is different from the others. In essence, he is happy. A conundrum in this place of disability and death—the nursing home. His capacity to enjoy seems oddly to have increased instead of diminished. I don't know what part of the brain controls enthusiasm, but for him this area is strangely enlarged, childlike even. He laughs at many things these days, something I don't remember him doing a lot before.

As the daily sister on his ward I know him well. And, living in the same village, I have known him a much longer time than these, his helpless days.

His wife has also noticed the change. She laughs a tinkling laugh as she tells me that it is quite strange that he can now sing in tune, whereas before he had no sense of pitch or tone. We joke together about some deep part of his brain having been mysteriously switched on to make up for the loss of the rest of his grey matter.

I often wonder what is going on in his mind. For wondering is often all you are left with after a stroke robs the power of speech. You fill in the gaps somehow or are just left guessing; and right or wrong that is the best you can do.

I have listened so many times to his wife tell me of conversations that she claims to have had with him. And I have said nothing; God knows she must need a little denial to get through the day. She believes the best, not because she is a coward. Quite simply, for her, he is still the man she married, the love of her life. She threads her fingers through his, touching his face with reverent grace.

The dining room, bedrooms and corridors are lined with dedicated carers; encouraging a few extra haltering steps, another reluctant mouthful of food. Some carers are subtly pained, with listless empty eyes as they tend their loved ones. Some mourn the lost spirit of the living physical body, and others the mind when their loved one no longer knows who they are.

Not so for Gwen, as she combs his few stray strands of hair with careful hand, watched by his alert and knowing eyes. I realize that for her he is still husband; friend. However, she is also a realist, a nurse like me, and she faces each day with a mixture of pleasure and grief in his company when he has good days and bad days.

But here today, watching them side by side, I see something new, something wonderful. Gently he caresses her hand with his good left hand. The hand that is not clawed and useless. He looks into her eyes and communicates a lifetime together. Now I understand why it is so hard for her to let go, to 'take a night off'.

He is still here.

He looks at his watch often. At the time the concert is due to finish he becomes a little agitated and gestures to a passing nurse. His chair had been hastily put in the hallway to cram the residents in for the concert. It is nearly time to clear the room and he doesn't want to be in anyone's way. Then I remember him as a man who always thought of others.

Vigilantly watching those around him, he acknowledges old friends with a 'yes, too long'. He does not shrink in embarrassment at his obvious disabilities but freely offers his good left hand for others to shake. He answers their awkward questions of 'How are you?' with an emphatic 'good'. He listens to their woes and responds with a measured 'Oh dear, too bad'.

Now I understand his language; their language. I understand why Gwen always asks him what he wants rather than talks about him as if he isn't there. She is a genius. A gifted, compassionate genius.

The conversation is not stimulating or riveting but it has a charm of its own. It is a tango, the dance of words, of love.

She poses the same question she asks every day, 'Do you want me to come back tonight?'

I have to stop myself from rushing in to tell her not to ask him. I feel she needs a break, a free night. But he says the predictable *'my word'* and she holds his hand against her face and sighs with contentment. It is their own gentle tango of love.